TURTLE TROUBLE

Turtle Trouble

Requests for information should be addressed to:

Zondervan, *Grand Rapids, Michigan 49530*

Library of Congress Cataloging-in-Publication Data

Avery, Ben, 1974–
Turtle Trouble / story by Ben Avery; art by Adi Darda
p. cm. -- (TimeFlyz; v. 2)
Includes bibliographical references and index.
ISBN-13: 978-0-310-71362-3 (pbk. : alk. paper)
ISBN-10: 0-310-71362-5 (pbk. : alk. paper)
1. Graphic novels. I. Adi Darda, 1972- II. Title.
PN6727.A945T87 2007
741.5'973--dc22

2007003756

Series Editor: Bud Rogers
Managing Editor: Bruce Nuffer
Managing Art Director: Merit Alderink

Printed in the United States of America

---

07 08 09 10 11 12 • 10 9 8 7 6 5 4 3 2 1

GRAPHIC NO

TURTLE TROUBLE

SERIES EDITOR:
BUD ROGERS

STORY BY BEN AVERY

ART BY ADI DARDA GAUDIAMO

ZONDERVAN.com/
AUTHORTRACKER
follow your favorite authors

CHAPTER ONE
NEAR BALTIMORE, MARYLAND. 1753.
TIK

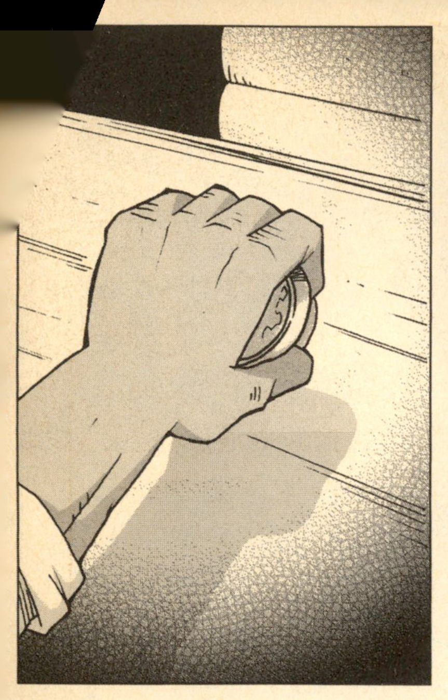

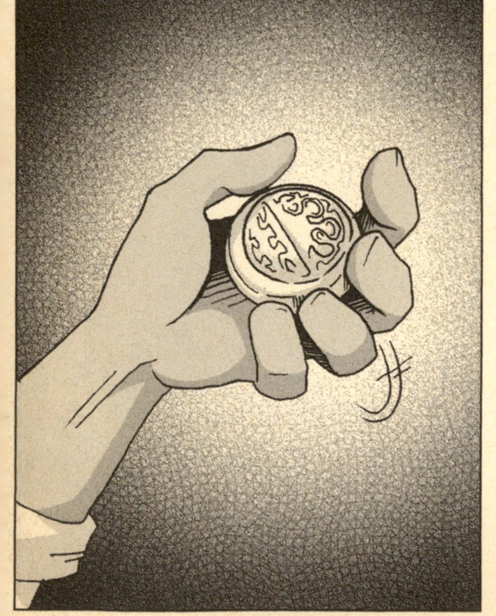

KNOCK!
KNOCK!
KNOCK!

WHO IS IT?

BENJAMIN...
IT IS GETTING LATE AND FATHER WANTS TO KNOW--

I'M WORKING, MINTA!
NO ONE IS TO BOTHER ME HERE!
BUT FATHER--
FATHER NEED NOT WORRY ABOUT HIS FARM!

UNDER MY GUIDANCE, THE CROPS HAVE BEEN THE BEST IN THE COUNTY, AND I WILL MAKE SURE THAT CONTINUES!
I WILL DO FATHER'S WORK TOMORROW!
HE KNOWS THAT!
BUT TONIGHT, I DO *MY* WORK!

YOU NEED REST!
I NEED QUIET!
THAT'S WHY I WORK OUT HERE AND NOT IN THE HOUSE!
YOU KNOW, YOU'VE ALMOST--ALMOST, BUT NOT QUITE--CREATED A FARM THAT CAN TAKE OF ITSELF...
...YOUR IRRIGATION, THE SOIL ROTATION, EVERYTHING YOU'VE DONE SINCE YOU TOOK OVER THE FARM WHEN YOU WERE FIFTEEN.
BUT AIN'T NO FARM CAN CARE FOR ITSELF. THIS FARM NEEDS YOU!

YOU AIN'T A CLOCK MAKER.
YOU'RE A FARMER.

MINTA... I'M SORRY. COME HERE.
I WANT YOU TO SEE SOMETHING.

NOW, I'VE STILL GOT TO FIGURE OUT THE BEST COUNTER-BALANCE...
...AND SINCE I'M JUST USING A KNIFE, GETTING THE COGS AND GEARS TO FIT JUST RIGHT HAS BEEN A MIGHT DIFFICULT...
...BUT IT WILL STRIKE ON THE SIX AND ON THE TWELVE, AND IT'LL BE AS PRECISE AS ANY FANCY SWISS CLOCK EVER'D BE!

BENJAMIN BANNEKER, DON'T YOU DARE...
...DON'T YOU DARE LISTEN TO A WORD WE SAY.

YOU KEEP THAT BRAIN OF YOURS WORKING AND FRESH.
YOU KEEP THAT MIND OF YOURS WOUND LIKE A CLOCK SO IT DON'T NEVER STOP WORKING, YOU HEAR?

I CANT BELIEVE IT...
...BOY IS A GENIUS AT EVERYTHING HE TOUCHES...

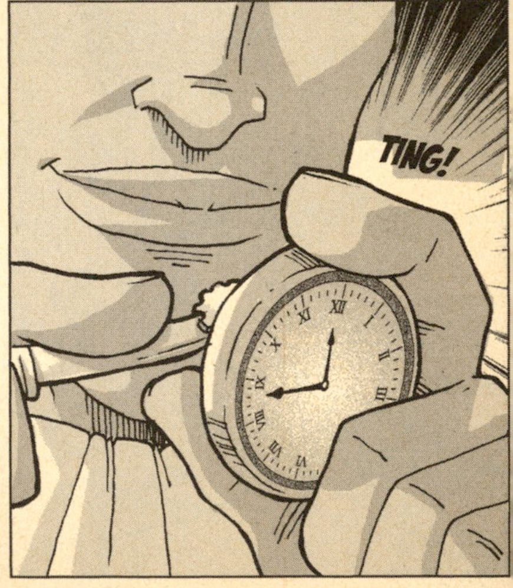
TING!

HMMMM...
YES...

WONDERFUL. BEAUTIFUL.
IT ALL MOVES SO PERFECTLY... LIKE A GIANT CLOCK WOUND INTO MOTION AGES AGO.
AND ONE DAY, I'M GOING TO FIGURE OUT HOW *THAT* CLOCK WORKS--

HUHN?

THE HUDSON RIVER. 1776.
SPLOOSH!

TIMES I THINK ABOUT MY NAME.
SLIPSTREAM.
STATUS, WORMHOLE?
UNSURE, SLIPSTREAM...
A SLIPSTREAM IS LIKE A TRAIL OF AIR LEFT BEHIND BY A FAST-MOVING OBJECT.
AND I DO HAVE TO MOVE FAST.

YET AGAIN N.E.X.U.S. HAS POOCHED OUT ON US!
I WARNED YOU!
IF WE HADN'T MADE THOSE EXTRA STOPS, MAYBE...
TO THE LEADER OF THIS SMALL GROUP OF FLIES CHASING THE EVIL DARCHON, SLOWING DOWN MEANS FAILING.
MAYBE WHAT?
NOTHING!
AND FAILING MEANS DARCHON AND HIS MASTER -- WHOEVER IT IS -- WIN.
THOUGHT SO!
BULLY...
SO IT FALLS ON MY SHOULDERS TO BRING THESE FLIES TOGETHER AS A SINGLE UNIT.

WHAT DID YOU SAY?
NOTHING!
BRINGING THEM TOGETHER ISN'T ALWAYS EASY. BUT I HAVE TO DO IT...
I AM NOT A BULLY!
AND IF YOU SAY IT AGAIN, I'LL--
OKAY, ENOUGH, GUYS!
WE'VE GOT A JOB TO DO!
DARCHON'S A TRICKY LITTLE SPIDER, AND HE'S NOT GOING TO WASTE ANY TIME HERE!
WE SHOULDN'T EITHER!
BECAUSE FAILURE IS NOT AN OPTION.

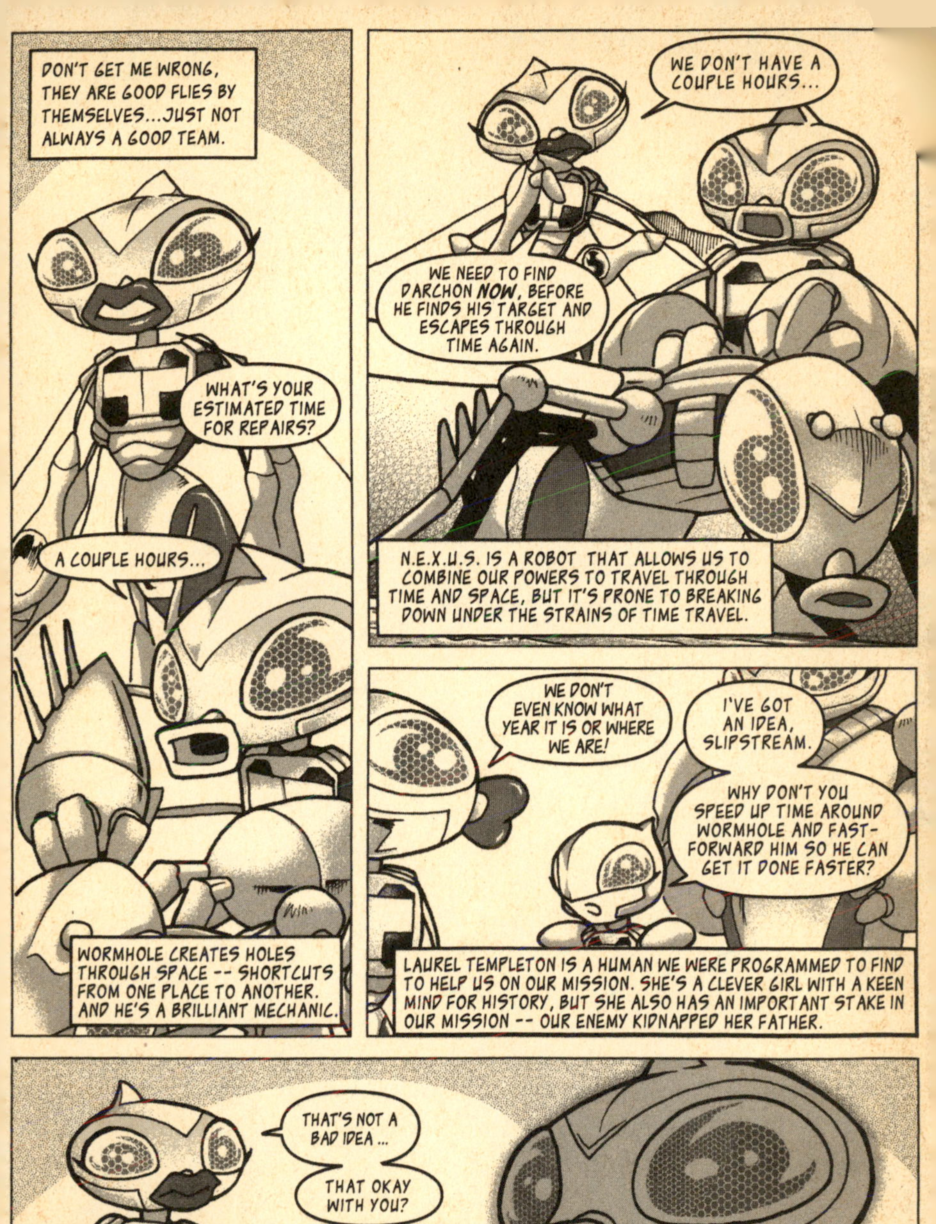
DON'T GET ME WRONG, THEY ARE GOOD FLIES BY THEMSELVES...JUST NOT ALWAYS A GOOD TEAM.
WHAT'S YOUR ESTIMATED TIME FOR REPAIRS?
A COUPLE HOURS...
WORMHOLE CREATES HOLES THROUGH SPACE -- SHORTCUTS FROM ONE PLACE TO ANOTHER. AND HE'S A BRILLIANT MECHANIC.
WE DON'T HAVE A COUPLE HOURS...
WE NEED TO FIND DARCHON NOW, BEFORE HE FINDS HIS TARGET AND ESCAPES THROUGH TIME AGAIN.
N.E.X.U.S. IS A ROBOT THAT ALLOWS US TO COMBINE OUR POWERS TO TRAVEL THROUGH TIME AND SPACE, BUT IT'S PRONE TO BREAKING DOWN UNDER THE STRAINS OF TIME TRAVEL.
WE DON'T EVEN KNOW WHAT YEAR IT IS OR WHERE WE ARE!
I'VE GOT AN IDEA, SLIPSTREAM.
WHY DON'T YOU SPEED UP TIME AROUND WORMHOLE AND FAST-FORWARD HIM SO HE CAN GET IT DONE FASTER?
LAUREL TEMPLETON IS A HUMAN WE WERE PROGRAMMED TO FIND TO HELP US ON OUR MISSION. SHE'S A CLEVER GIRL WITH A KEEN MIND FOR HISTORY, BUT SHE ALSO HAS AN IMPORTANT STAKE IN OUR MISSION -- OUR ENEMY KIDNAPPED HER FATHER.
THAT'S NOT A BAD IDEA ...
THAT OKAY WITH YOU?
FINE BY ME!

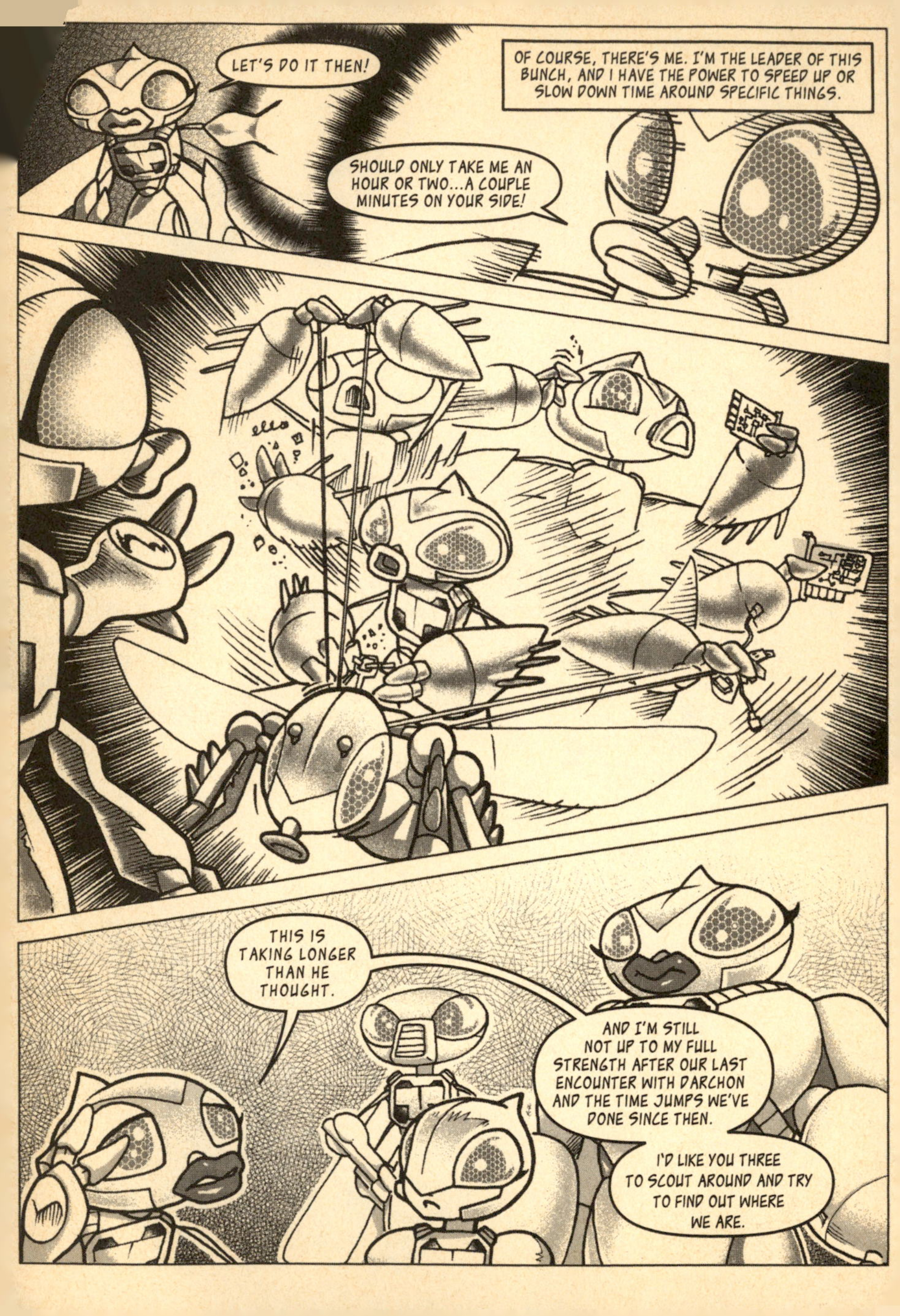
LET'S DO IT THEN!
OF COURSE, THERE'S ME. I'M THE LEADER OF THIS BUNCH, AND I HAVE THE POWER TO SPEED UP OR SLOW DOWN TIME AROUND SPECIFIC THINGS.
SHOULD ONLY TAKE ME AN HOUR OR TWO...A COUPLE MINUTES ON YOUR SIDE!
THIS IS TAKING LONGER THAN HE THOUGHT.
AND I'M STILL NOT UP TO MY FULL STRENGTH AFTER OUR LAST ENCOUNTER WITH DARCHON AND THE TIME JUMPS WE'VE DONE SINCE THEN.
I'D LIKE YOU THREE TO SCOUT AROUND AND TRY TO FIND OUT WHERE WE ARE.

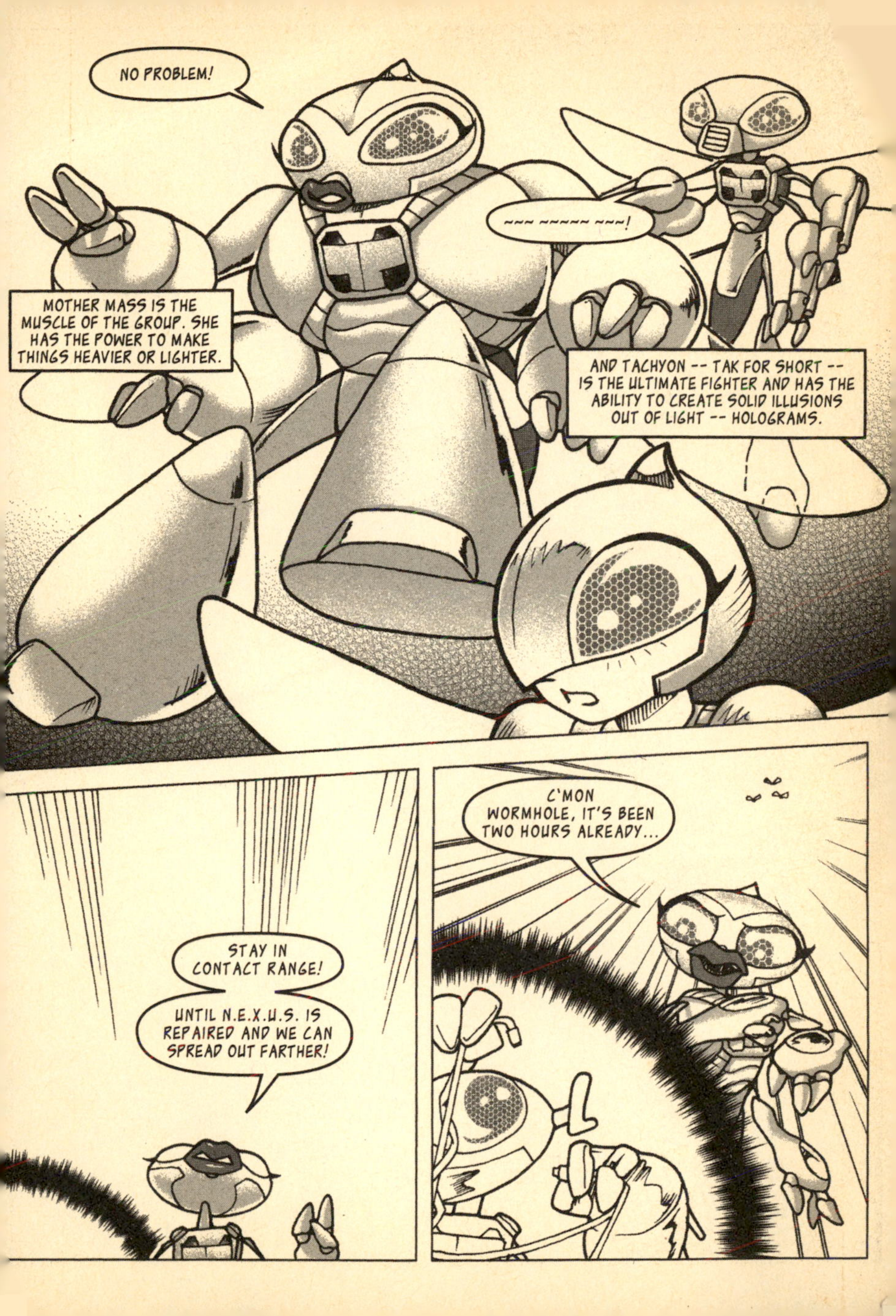
NO PROBLEM!
~~~ ~~~~~~ ~~~!
MOTHER MASS IS THE MUSCLE OF THE GROUP. SHE HAS THE POWER TO MAKE THINGS HEAVIER OR LIGHTER.
AND TACHYON -- TAK FOR SHORT -- IS THE ULTIMATE FIGHTER AND HAS THE ABILITY TO CREATE SOLID ILLUSIONS OUT OF LIGHT -- HOLOGRAMS.
STAY IN CONTACT RANGE!
UNTIL N.E.X.U.S. IS REPAIRED AND WE CAN SPREAD OUT FARTHER!
C'MON WORMHOLE, IT'S BEEN TWO HOURS ALREADY...
~~~

ANY IDEAS YET, KIDDO?
NO...
BUT WE SHOULD FOLLOW THIS RIVER DOWNSTREAM.
WE'RE BOUND TO FIND SOME SORT OF CITY OR VILLAGE.
SO I MOVE FAST AND HOPE THEY CAN FOLLOW MY TRAIL -- MY "SLIPSTREAM."
BECAUSE FAILURE IS NOT AN OPTION.

HEY. KIDDO, UH, I GOT A QUESTION.
I'M NOT A BULLY, AM I?
YOU'RE VERY KIND TO ME --
THANK YOU!
BUT...
BUT?
...YOU CAN BE A LITTLE TOUGH ON WORMHOLE.
THAT'S NOT BULLYING!
THAT'S...
...TOUGH LOVE!
UH, I NEED TO CHECK ON SOMETHING UP HERE...

HMMMM...

HEY, YOU DON'T THINK I'M A BULLY, DO YOU?
~~ ~~~~~~ ~~ ~~~.

FWOOSH
WELL, THAT WAS RUDE!
HEY, GUYS!

I FOUND OUR FIRST CLUE AS TO WHERE AND WHEN WE ARE.

ME AND PA WENT DOWN TO CAMP ALONG WITH CAPTAIN GOODING! AND THERE WE SEEN THE MEN AND BOYS AS THICK AS HASTY PUDDING!
AND THERE WE SEEN A SWAMPIN' GUN, LARGE AS A LOG OF MAPLE, UPON A BLASTED LITTLE CART, A LOAD OF FATHER'S CATTLE!
AND EVERY TIME THEY SHOOT IT OFF, IT TAKES A HORN OF POWDER; IT MAKES A NOISE LIKE FATHER'S GUN, ONLY A NATION LOUDER.
I KNOW THAT TUNE...

AND THERE WAS CAPTAIN WASHINGTON, AND GENTLEMAN ABOUT HIM: THEY SAY HE'S GROWN SO BLASTED PROUD, HE WILL NOT RIDE WITHOUT 'EM.
THERE WAS CAPTAIN WASHINGTON UPON A SLAPPING STALLION A-GIVING ORDERS TO HIS MEN I GUESS THERE WAS A MIL--
--SHOO!-- --MILLION!
I THINK I KNOW WHERE WE ARE... OR AT LEAST WHEN!

THERE CAME GEN'RAL WASHINGTON UPON A SNOW-WHITE CHARGER ♫ ♫
♫ HE LOOKED AS BIG AS ALL OUTDOORS AND THOUGHT THAT HE WAS LARGER. ♫
CLICK!
SLIPSTREAM, LAUREL THINKS SHE KNOWS WHERE WE ARE!
THAT'S GREAT! WHERE?
YANKEE DOODLE KEEP IT UP, YANKEE DOODLE DANDY ♫ MIND THE MUSIC AND THE STEP, AND WITH THE GIRLS BE HANDY! ♫
WELL, I THINK...
...SOMETIME AROUND THE REVOLUTIONARY WAR, IN THE AMERICAN COLONIES!

THAT'S GREAT TO KNOW!
SOOOO...WHEN IS THAT?
THE 1770'S... ALMOST TWO HUNDRED AND FIFTY YEARS AGO!
MAYBE FOR YOU!
WHAT DO YOU MEAN?
ARE YOU GUYS FROM THE FUTURE?
YOU NEVER TOLD ME.
TRUTH IS, WE DON'T KNOW *WHEN* WE'RE FROM.
WHAT DO YOU MEAN?
JUST THAT. WE DON'T KNOW WHEN OR WHERE WE WERE CREATED. IN YOUR FUTURE OR IN YOUR PAST -- WE DON'T KNOW.

WHEW, CAN'T KEEP IT UP ANY LONGER...
SO ANYWAY, WHILE YOU MIGHT CALL THIS TWO HUNDRED AND FIFTY YEARS IN THE PAST, I JUST CONSIDER IT A DIFFERENT NOW!
THAT MAKES SENSE... I THINK...
GLAD IT MAKES SENSE TO YOU, 'CAUSE I CAN'T MAKE HEAD NOR TAILS OF ANY OF THAT!
OOOOOH! ♫
YANKEE DOODLE KEEP IT UP, YANKEE DOODLE DANDY ♫ MIND THE MUSIC AND THE STEP, ♫ AND WITH THE GIRLS BE HAAAANDEEEE!
COME NOW, WE MAY KNOW WHERE WE ARE, BUT WE DON'T KNOW WHAT DARCHON IS AFTER HERE.
~~~~ ~~ ~~~~ ~~~~!
RIGHT! KEEP MOVING!
~~~~

I'M HUNGRY! HOW LONG WAS I WORKING?
ABOUT FIFTEEN MINUTES, OUR TIME.
FELT LIKE NINE HOURS!
CLOSER TO SEVEN.
ARE YOU GOING TO BE ABLE TO FIX THAT THING?
SOME OF ITS WIRING MELTED, BUT I WAS ABLE TO REWIRE IT. I THINK.
RIGHT...
IT'S ALMOST DONE...
JUST A LITTLE TWEAKING HERE AND THERE...

OUR ENEMY IS DARCHON, ALTHOUGH IT WASN'T UNTIL WE HAD LAUREL IN OUR LITTLE GROUP THAT WE FINALLY STARTED LEARNING ABOUT HIM.
HMMMM...
SO NOT ONLY ARE THEY WEAKENED FROM THEIR TRAVEL, BUT THEIR ROBOT IS DOWN AS WELL.
MEANING, THEY CANNOT SENSE WHEN I AM USING MY OWN POWER.
AND THEY HAVE NO IDEA WHO MY TARGET MIGHT BE.
I STILL HAVE THE ELEMENT OF SURPRISE.
SO THE QUESTION COMES...
...WHAT TO DO TO TAKE ADVANTAGE OF THIS DEVELOPMENT?
HERE'S WHAT WE *DO* KNOW...

HE HAS A COMBINATION OF ALL OUR POWERS ...
SILLY BEAST, YOU CANNOT EAT SOMEONE WHO CAN MAKE YOU LIGHTER THAN AIR!
BUT, YOU HAVE GIVEN ME AN IDEA ...
???
!!!

... AND PROBABLY SOME POWERS WE DON'T EVEN KNOW ABOUT.
HEHEHEH ...

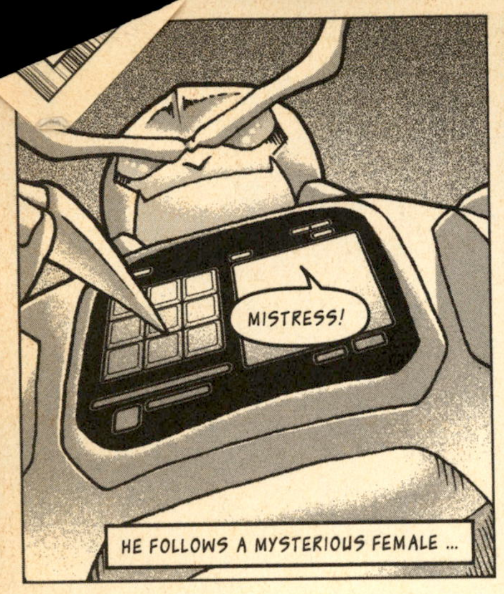
MISTRESS!
HE FOLLOWS A MYSTERIOUS FEMALE ...

DARCHON, I TRUST THE FLIES HAVE NOT FOLLOWED YOU?

MISTRESS, THEY HAVE, BUT --
WHAT!!!

AGAIN YOU CONTACT ME WHEN THE FLIES HAVE FOLLOWED YOU!!!
AND EVEN RISKING VISUAL COMMUNICATION, WHICH GIVES OFF A STRONGER SIGNAL FOR THEM TO TRACE?!?
WE DON'T KNOW WHO OR WHAT SHE IS -- HUMAN? SPIDER? FLY? SOMETHING ELSE? -- BUT WE DO KNOW THIS ...

... SHE IS EVIL.
YOU ARE A FOOL, DARCHON!!!
IF THEY WERE TO TRACE OUR COMMUNICATION!?!
YOU'RE LITTLE MORE THAN A FOOLISH GOON!
MILADY, YOU DO NOT UNDERSTAND!
THEY HAVE FOLLOWED ME HERE -- ONCE AGAIN, QUITE CLOSELY ON MY TAIL, I MIGHT ADD --
BUT THE ROBOT, THE ONE THAT ALLOWS THEM TO USE THEIR POWERS TOGETHER, IS DAMAGED!
HMMM ...
AND HOW DO YOU PLAN TO USE THIS TO YOUR ADVANTAGE?
WHILE THEIR ROBOT IS DOWN, THEY CANNOT DETECT MY USE OF POWER.
AND WHILE THEY CANNOT DETECT MY USE OF POWER, I INTEND TO PREPARE AN ASSAULT THE LIKES OF WHICH THEY HAVE NEVER SEEN ...

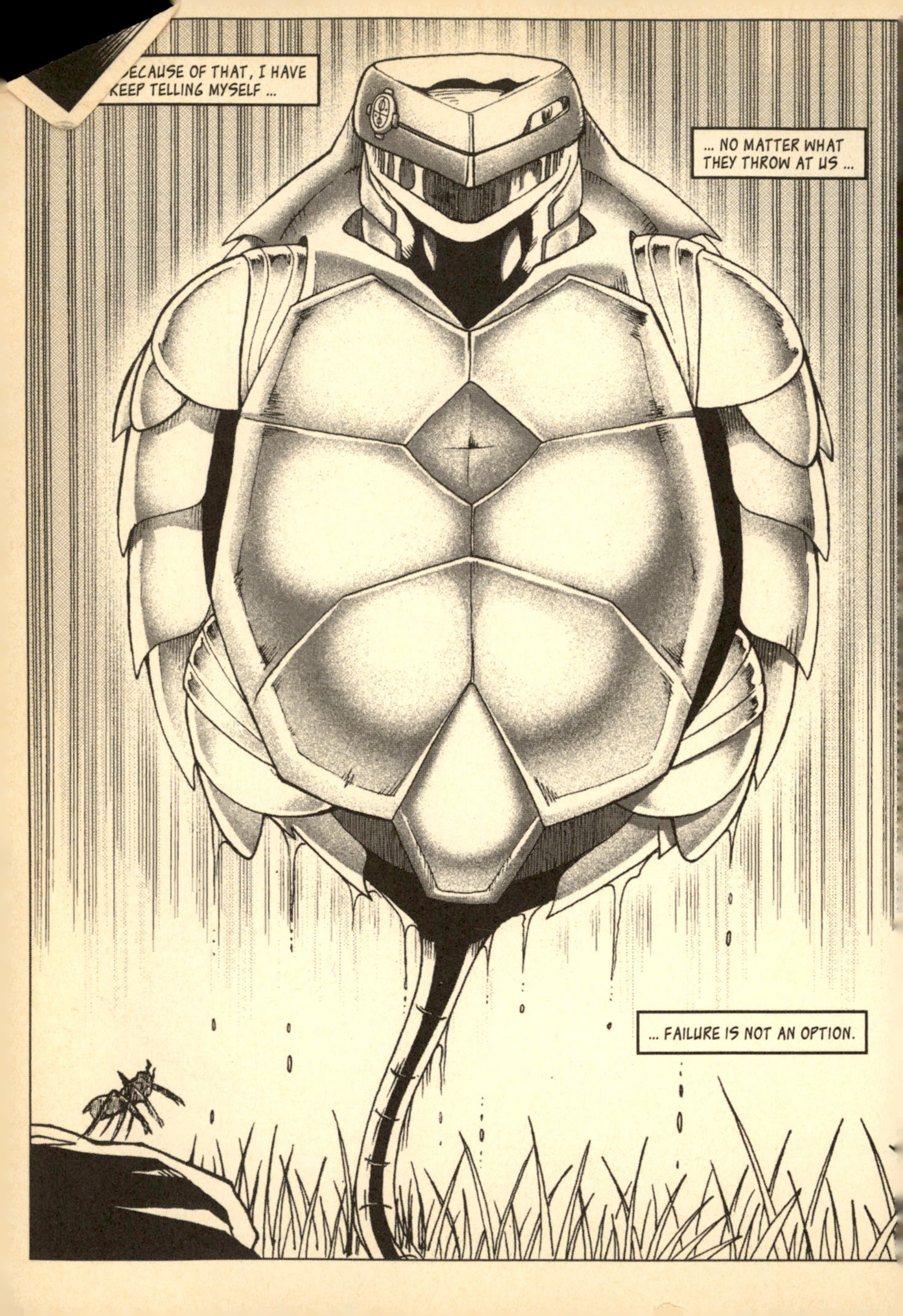
BECAUSE OF THAT, I HAVE
KEEP TELLING MYSELF ...
... NO MATTER WHAT THEY THROW AT US ...
... FAILURE IS NOT AN OPTION.

CHAPTER THREE
SO, WE KNOW WHEN WE ARE ...
IT SHOULD BE EASY TO FIND OUT WHERE WE ARE ...
THE HARD QUESTION IS WHO ARE WE HERE TO PROTECT?
UNFORTUNATELY, WHILE IT IS EASY FOR ME TO FOCUS ON OUR MISSION ...

... SOMETIMES MY TEAM FINDS IT A LITTLE HARDER TO STAY FOCUSED.
OOOO, THAT'S PRETTY ...

CHILD, WE'RE NOT HERE TO GO SHOPPING ...
... WE'RE HERE TO FIND WHAT GENIUS SCIENTIST DARCHON IS HERE TO KIDNAP!

ACTUALLY, IN A WAY, SHOPPING IS PART OF THE PLAN, SO TAK CAN CREATE A HOLOGRAPHIC COSTUME FOR ME. AND I CAN'T BE BLAMED FOR WANTING A PRETTY --
WHOA-HO-WOW!!!
I I I I ...

I THINK I KNOW WHO DARCHON'S AFTER ...
SOMETIMES, THEY FOCUS A LITTLE TOO MUCH ON THE WRONG THINGS.
AND THAT COSTS US.

I CAN'T BELIEVE THIS ...

THAT'S BENJAMIN FRANKLIN, ONE OF THE GREATEST AMERICAN INVENTORS TO EVER LIVE!

TAK, CAN YOU MAKE THAT DRESS FOR ME?
MAKE A HOLOGRAM LIKE THAT DRESS?
~~~ ~~~~ ~~~~!

DOESN'T SEEM TOO SMART, USING AN UMBRELLA AND IT'S NOT EVEN RAINING.
~~~

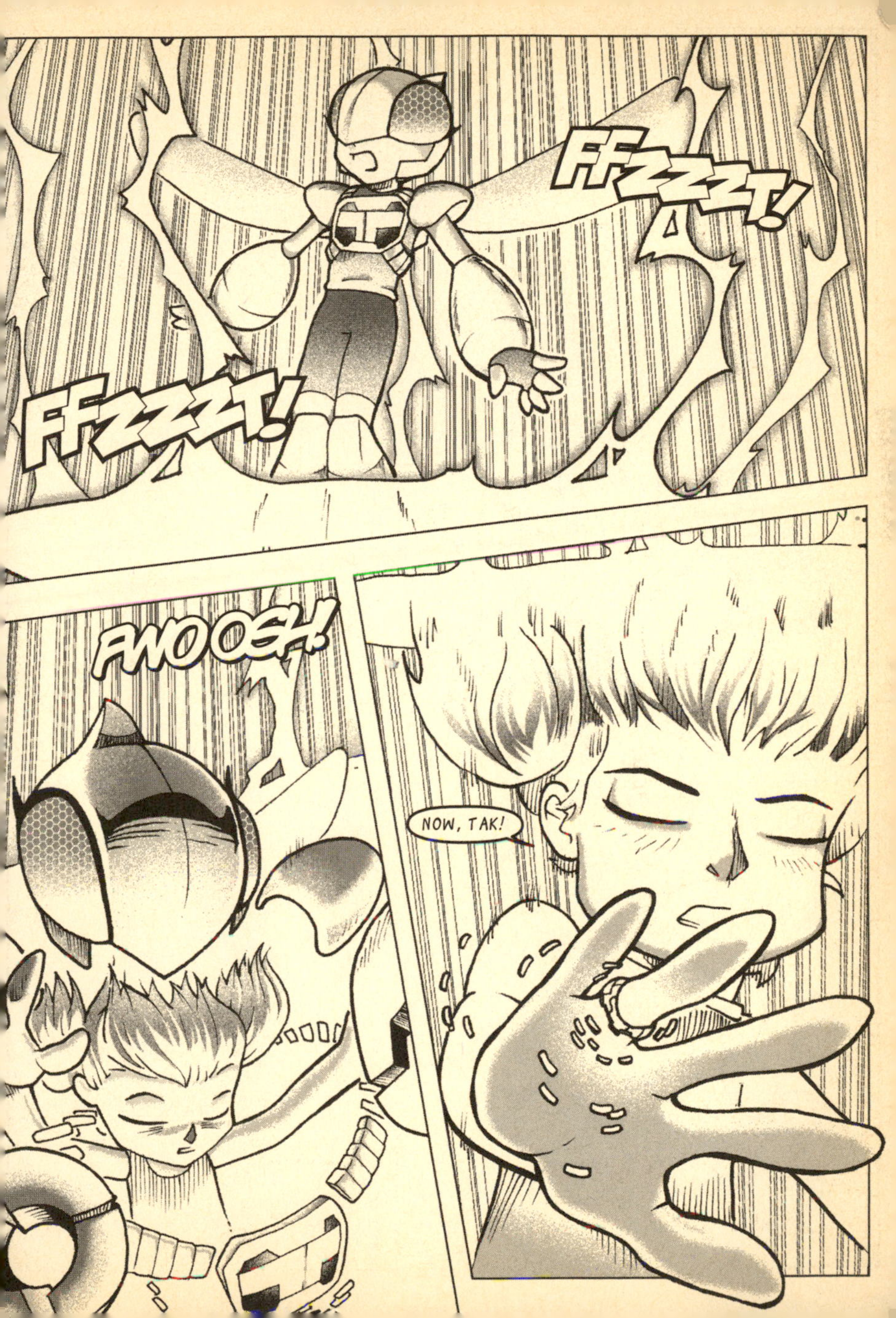
FFZZZZT!
FFZZZZT!
FWOOSH!
NOW, TAK!

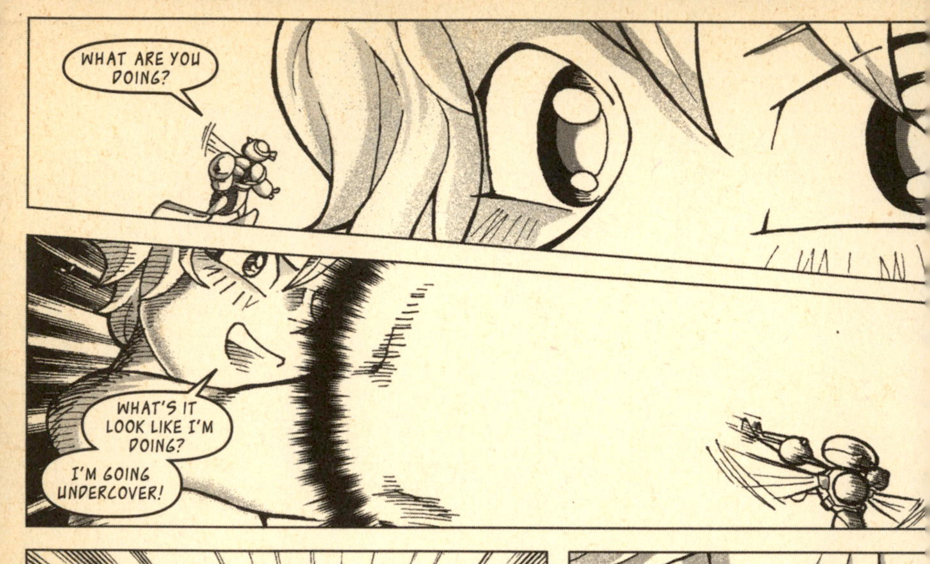
WHAT ARE YOU DOING?
WHAT'S IT LOOK LIKE I'M DOING?
I'M GOING UNDERCOVER!

GREAT JOB, TAK!
"GOING UNDERCOVER"?
DOESN'T THAT INVOLVE SOME SORT OF SNEAKING AROUND?

THAT'S WHY I HAD TAK MAKE ME THE COSTUME!
YEAH, BUT YOU GREW AND HAD TAK MAKE YOUR COSTUME ...

... IN THE MIDDLE OF THE STREET!
OOPS.

UH, TAK?
YOU THINK YOU COULD MAKE ME INVISIBLE?

FWOOSH!!
THANKS.

WAHL, THAT BEAT ALL!
SORRY ABOUT THAT ...
YOU SHOULD BE!
THAT WAS PRETTY STUPID, HUH?
DON'T DO IT AGAIN.
I GUESS I JUST GOT EXCITED ABOUT SEEING BENJAMIN FRANKLIN!
YOU CAN'T LET YOUR EXCITEMENT GET IN THE WAY OF YOUR BETTER JUDGMENT, CHILD.
WHAT'S GOING ON?
MAMA! THEM FLIES 'S TALKIN'!

OKAY, NOW THAT MY FOOLISHNESS IS OUT OF THE WAY, LET'S TRY THIS AGAIN.

PROBABLY SHOULD TRY SOMETHING A LITTLE LESS CONSPICUOUS THOUGH, TAK.

I MEAN, THIS DRESS IS BEAUTIFUL AND ALL, BUT MAYBE IT'S A LITTLE MUCH.

I'M TELLIN' YA, MA!
THEM FLIES WAS TALKIN'!
ENOUGH, JOHNNY! WAIT'LL I TELL YOUR FATHER ABOUT THE FIBS YOU'RE TELLING!
NOT AS FANCY, BUT THIS'LL DO.
NICE WORK, TAK.
NOW, LET'S GO FIND BENJAMIN FRANKLIN!

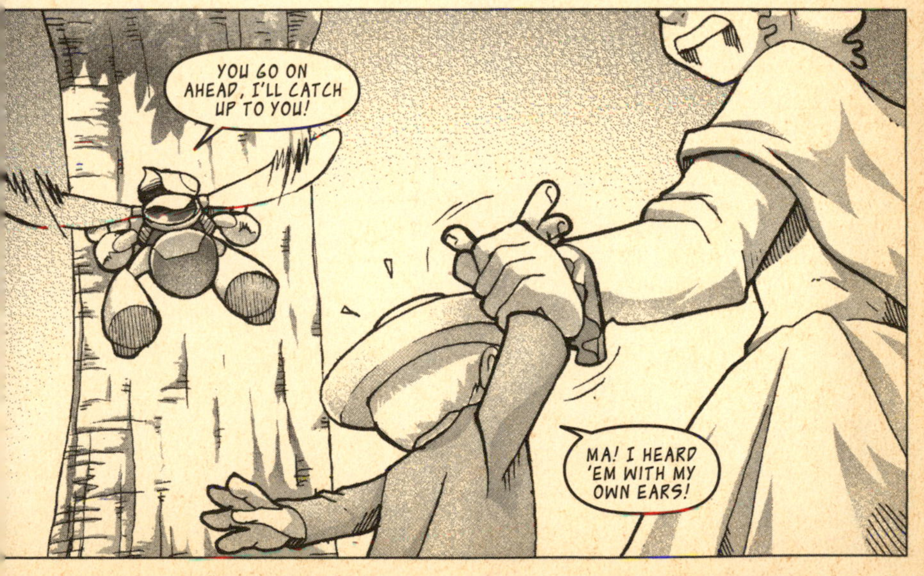
YOU GO ON AHEAD, I'LL CATCH UP TO YOU!
MA! I HEARD 'EM WITH MY OWN EARS!

I'M GONNA CLEAN THEM LIES OUT YOUR MOUTH WITH SOAP!
MA! I WAS LYIN' 'BOUT THE APPLE FROM MR. SMITH'S ORCHARD ...
AND THE ROCK PA FOUND IN HIS POTATOES ...
AND THE INK IN SISSY'S HAIR ...
BUT I AIN'T LYIN' TODAY!
NOW, YOU LISTEN HERE, JOHNNY --
EXCUSE ME!
YOUR BOY WASN'T LYING, MA'AM!
AND I HEARD YOU TELL YOUR MOTHER ABOUT ALL THOSE LIES YOU TOLD.
ALWAYS REMEMBER, THE TRUTH IS ALWAYS THE BEST ANSWER, GOT IT?

MA?
YES, JOHNNY?
YOU SEEN IT TALKIN', RIGHT, MA?
YES, JOHNNY. I BELIEVE YOU NOW.

JOHNNY?
YES, MA?
WE AIN'T GONNA TELL YOUR PA 'BOUT THIS, RIGHT, JOHNNY?
NO WAY, MA! AIN'T NO WAY HE'D BELIEVE THIS!

SEE, YOU'RE NOT A BULLY, MOTHER MASS!
YOU REALLY ARE KIND!

TO ME, ANYWAY ...
... AND TO THAT LITTLE BOY ...
... AND, WELL, TO ANYONE WHO ISN'T WORMHOLE.

HMMM, MAYBE I AM A LITTLE TOUGH ON THAT OLD BLOCKHEAD ...

I CAN'T BELIEVE THIS IS HAPPENING!
WHENEVER THEY ASK US WHO WE'D LIKE TO MEET IF WE COULD MEET ANYONE IN THE WORLD, MY FRIENDS ALWAYS SAID THINGS LIKE POP STARS OR TV STARS OR MOVIE STARS OR SPORTS STARS --
-- EXCEPT MY BROTHER. HE WANTED TO MEET MAYA ANGELOU --
-- BUT FOR ME, IT WAS ALWAYS ***BENJAMIN FRANKLIN!***
DID YOU KNOW THAT HE DISCOVERED THAT LIGHTNING WAS ACTUALLY ELECTRICITY?
HE WAS ALSO THE AMBASSADOR TO FRANCE ...
... AND HE INVENTED BIFOCAL GLASSES!
JUST THINK, MY GRANNY COULDN'T READ IF IT WASN'T FOR HIM!
AND HE HELPED WRITE THE DECLARATION OF INDEPENDENCE!

I HAVE ***SOOOO*** MANY QUESTIONS FOR HIM!
HE'S MY FAVORITE PERSON IN HISTORY, AND SINCE HE WAS A SCIENTIST, HE WAS ACTUALLY SOMEONE BOTH MY FATHER AND I COULD TALK ABOUT!
I'VE IMAGINED MEETING HIM EVER SINCE I WAS A LITTLE GIRL!
I'VE THOUGHT ABOUT ALL THE THINGS I'D LIKE TO ASK --
WUMP

WHOOOOOA-
OOOF!
WUMP
OH DEAR, MISS ...

ARE YOU OKAY?
...
...

HMMM, YOU STILL SEEM TO HAVE THE SPARK OF LIFE.
YOU'LL BE FINE.
NEXT TIME, THOUGH, YOU MAY WANT TO *WATCH* WHERE YOU'RE GOING.

...
...

YES, WELL, ADIEU ...

...
...
UH ...

NICE UMBRELLA!
...
REALLY? YOU THINK SO?
MOST THE PEOPLE AROUND HERE THINK I'M PRETTY SILLY FOR CARRYING IT.
IT'S SOMETHING I PICKED UP BACK IN FRANCE ... MEN AND WOMEN CARRY THEM THERE, AND NOT JUST FOR RAIN.
I TEND TO LIKE IT.

DO I KNOW YOU?
NO, OF COURSE NOT.
BUT I KNOW YOU!
YOU'RE BENJAMIN FRANKLIN!
YOU INVENTED THE FRANKLIN STOVE!
AND DISCOVERED ELECTRICITY IN LIGHTNING!
AND STARTED FIREHOUSE PROGRAMS!
AND INVENTED BIFOCALS!
AND SIGNED THE CONSTITUTION!
"CONSTITUTION"? "BIFOCALS"? YOU SEEM TO KNOW A LOT ABOUT ME, YOUNG LADY ...
... BUT I DON'T REMEMBER ANYTHING LIKE THAT ...

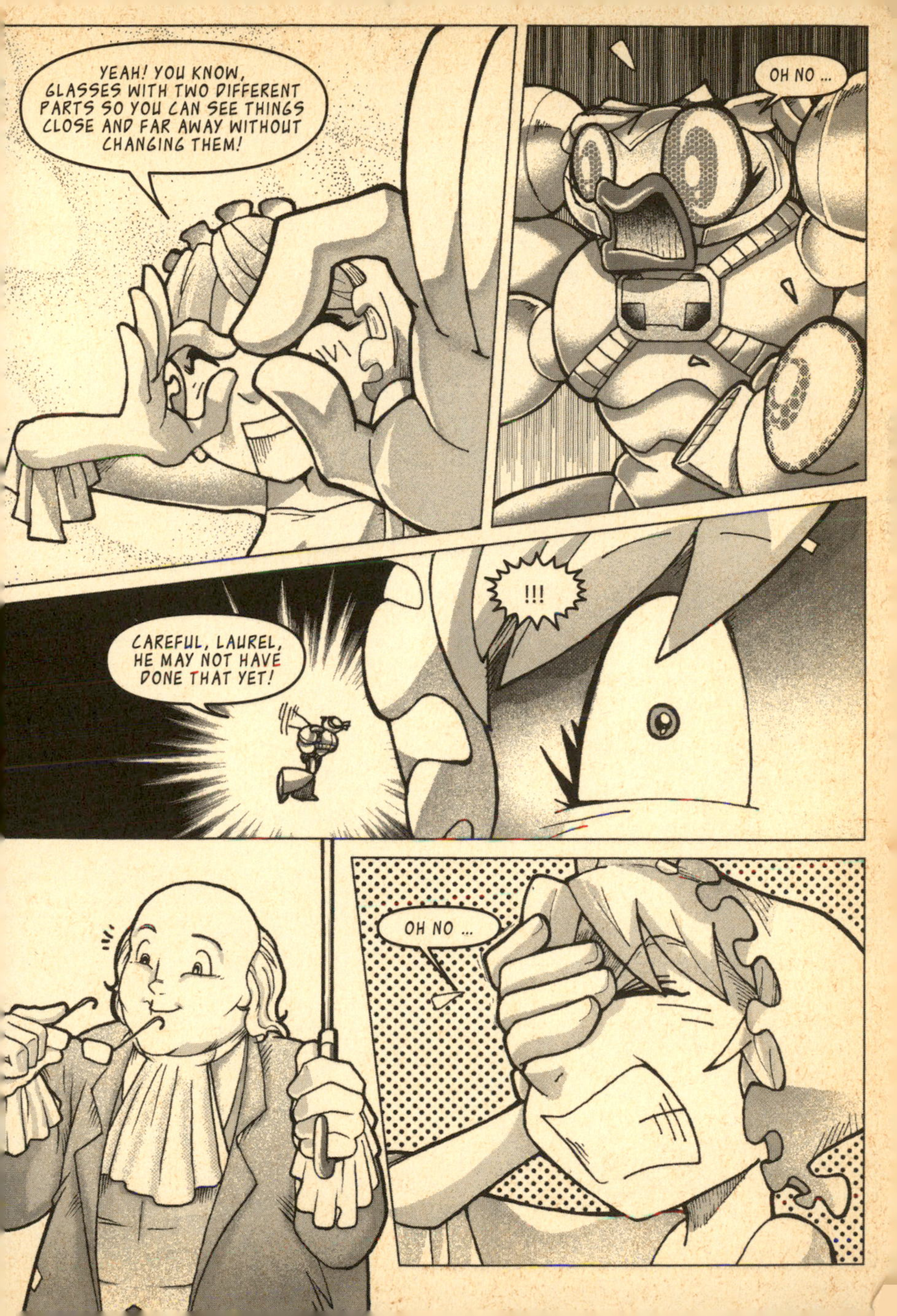
YEAH! YOU KNOW, GLASSES WITH TWO DIFFERENT PARTS SO YOU CAN SEE THINGS CLOSE AND FAR AWAY WITHOUT CHANGING THEM!
OH NO ...
!!!
CAREFUL, LAUREL, HE MAY NOT HAVE DONE THAT YET!
OH NO ...

WELL, YOUNG LADY, WHAT'S YOUR NAME?
LAUREL. LAUREL TEMPLETON.
WELL, MISS TEMPLETON, I'M PLEASED YOU KNOW SO MUCH ABOUT ME.
WOULD YOU LIKE TO MEET A COLLEAGUE OF MINE? HE'S ALSO AN INVENTOR.
SURE! I'D LOVE TO!
BUT YOU'RE NOT JUST ONE PERSON, YOU'RE THE FIRST AND GREATEST AMERICAN SCIENTIST EVER!!!
"NICE UMBRELLA"?
I'VE WAITED ALL MY LIFE TO SAY THAT!?!
HEHEH!
~ ~~~ ~!

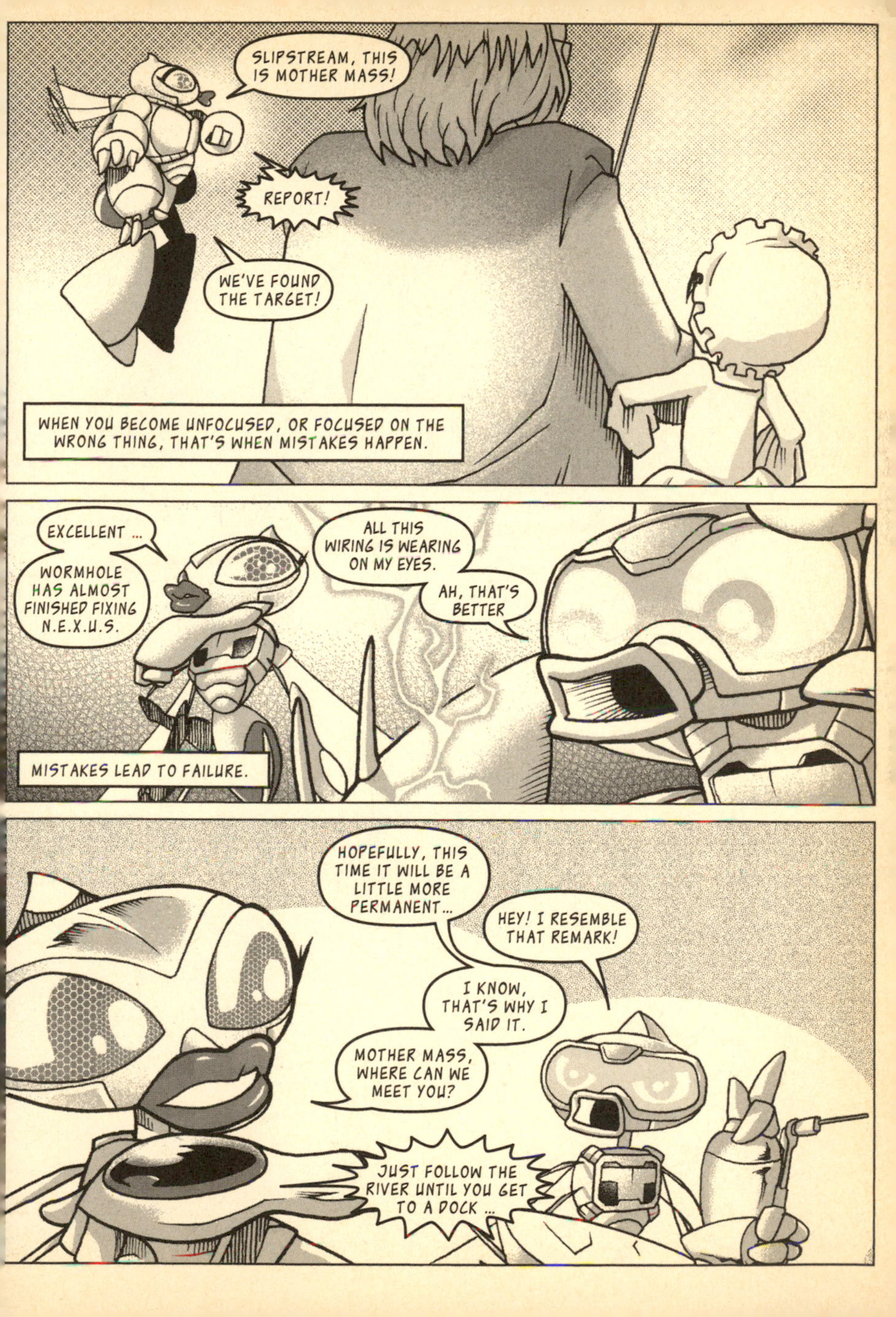
SLIPSTREAM, THIS IS MOTHER MASS!
REPORT!
WE'VE FOUND THE TARGET!
WHEN YOU BECOME UNFOCUSED, OR FOCUSED ON THE WRONG THING, THAT'S WHEN MISTAKES HAPPEN.
EXCELLENT ...
WORMHOLE HAS ALMOST FINISHED FIXING N.E.X.U.S.
ALL THIS WIRING IS WEARING ON MY EYES.
AH, THAT'S BETTER
MISTAKES LEAD TO FAILURE.
HOPEFULLY, THIS TIME IT WILL BE A LITTLE MORE PERMANENT...
HEY! I RESEMBLE THAT REMARK!
I KNOW, THAT'S WHY I SAID IT.
MOTHER MASS, WHERE CAN WE MEET YOU?
JUST FOLLOW THE RIVER UNTIL YOU GET TO A DOCK ...

MISS TEMPLETON, MAY I INTRODUCE YOU TO MR. DAVID BUSHNELL AND HIS SUBMERSIBLE BATTLESHIP --
I CALL IT THE TURTLE!
... WITH A WEIRD LOOKING LITTLE BOAT.
AND WE WERE ABOUT TO MAKE ONE OF OUR BIGGEST MISTAKES YET ...

MR. FRANKLIN!
GOOD TO SEE YOU!
I WOULDN'T MISS THIS DAY FOR ANYTHING, DAVID.

THIS YOUNG MAN, MISS TEMPLETON, IS NAUGHT BUT A YEAR OUT OF YALE, AND ALREADY HE'S TAKING COMMISSIONED WORK FROM GENERAL WASHINGTON HIMSELF!
NOW, MR. FRANKLIN, PLEASE, YOU'RE EMBARRASSING ME!

AND PLEASE, CALL ME BENJAMIN.
WE ARE PEERS, MY FRIEND.
I TRUST THE BIOLUMINESCENT FUNGUS WORKED?
"BIOLUMINESCENT FUNGUS"? SOUNDS PRETTY GROSS ...

YOUNG LADY, WITHOUT MR. FRANKLIN -- ER, BENJAMIN -- AND HIS FUNGUS, MY INVENTION WOULD NEVER HAVE WORKED!

MY BOAT ACTUALLY GOES UNDER WATER, SO NO ONE CAN SEE IT COMING!
COMPLETELY WATERPROOF!

PHEWF!
ONE PROBLEM: IN THE DAYTIME YOU CAN STILL SEE IT COMING, SO WE NEED TO USE THE TURTLE AT NIGHT ...
WORKS BEST AT NIGHT!

BUT THE SAME THING THAT GIVES US COVER -- NIGHT'S DARKNESS --MAKES SEEING THE CONTROLS IMPOSSIBLE.
TOO DARK TO SEE!

WE COULDN'T USE AN OPEN FIRE BECAUSE IT WOULD BURN UP ALL THE BREATHABLE AIR!
NO AIR = NO BREATH = BAD!

I THOUGHT ABOUT COLLECTING A JAR FULL OF FIREFLIES.
WAY TOO MUCH WORK!

THEN I GOT IT!
I'D ASK THE MOST RESPECTED INVENTOR IN ALL THE COLONIES TO HELP WITH MY INVENTION! BENJAMIN FRANKLIN!
IT'S 1776! THE LIGHT BULB WASN'T INVENTED YET!

HE THOUGHT ABOUT IT FOR A WHILE AND CAME UP WITH AN IDEA!
MUSHROOMS!

BUT NOT JUST ANY MUSHROOMS!
MR. FRANK-- BENJAMIN -- KNEW OF SOME MUSHROOMS THAT GLOWED IN THE DARK!

AND NOW, WELL, HERE WE ARE, ABOUT TO TAKE MY TURTLE INTO BATTLE FOR THE FIRST TIME EVER!
OH, HEY LITTLE GUY!'
GLAD TO SEE YOU GOT FIXED!
BZZT!!!
I MEAN ... SHOO, FLY!
WHUT'S GOIN' ON HERE!

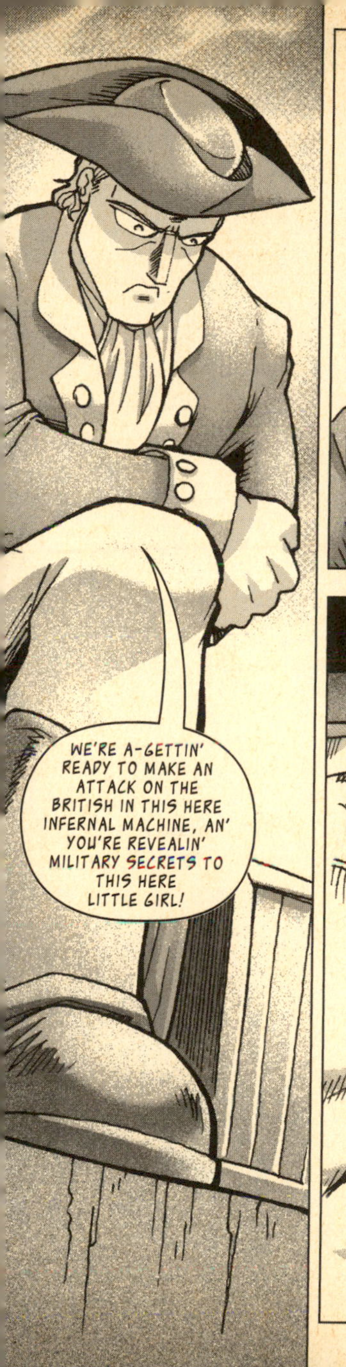
WE'RE A-GETTIN' READY TO MAKE AN ATTACK ON THE BRITISH IN THIS HERE INFERNAL MACHINE, AN' YOU'RE REVEALIN' MILITARY SECRETS TO THIS HERE LITTLE GIRL!

YOU THINK YOU'RE ALL SMART AS A STEEL TRAP, BUT I AIN'T SEEIN' IT!
NOW, LISTEN, I, UH ... YOU KNOW ...
I BROUGHT THE GIRL.

WHO'RE YOU?
I'M BENJAMIN FRANKLIN. FRIEND AND ADVISOR TO MR. BUSHNELL HERE.
I HELPED HIM WITH THIS CONTRAPTION AND THE YOUNG LADY IS WITH ME.
OH. UH. HMMP.

MAY I INTRODUCE TO YOU SERGEANT EZRA LEE OF THE CONTINENTAL ARMY.
HE'S GOING TO PILOT THE TURTLE.
THAT'S RIGHT. JUST POINT ME IN THE DI-RECTION OF THEM RED COATS AND WATCH THE SPARKS FLY!

WELL, I EXPECT THERE WILL BE MORE THAN ... MORE THAN JUST SPARKS.
MR. BUSHNELL, WHY CAN'T *YOU* JUST DRIVE YOUR SUBMARINE?
I UH, I WOULD, BUT, UM, I'M TOO ...
NEEDS A BIG STRONG MAN TO DO THE JOB FOR 'IM!

THAT MAN'D BE ME!

DAVID'S BROTHER WAS GOING TO PILOT THE TURTLE.
HE HAD TRAINED AND WAS READY TO TAKE IT INTO BATTLE, BUT HE GOT SICK.
OH, I HOPE HE'S GOING TO BE OKAY ...
NO.
HE'S NOT GOING TO GET BETTER, IF THAT'S WHAT YOU MEAN.
MY BROTHER DIED.
I'M SORRY ...
THERE WAS NOTHING ANYONE COULD DO.
IT HAPPENS, ESPECIALLY HERE IN THE COLONIES.
AND I KNOW THAT MY BROTHER IS IN A PLACE WHERE THERE IS NO PAIN...
... NO WAR ...

YEAH, YEAH, YEAH!
BUT NOW WE GOT US A BATTLE TA WIN!
SO SNAP OUT OF IT!
SLAP!
HE ALWAYS GETS LIKE THIS WHEN WE TALK ABOUT HIS BROTHER ...

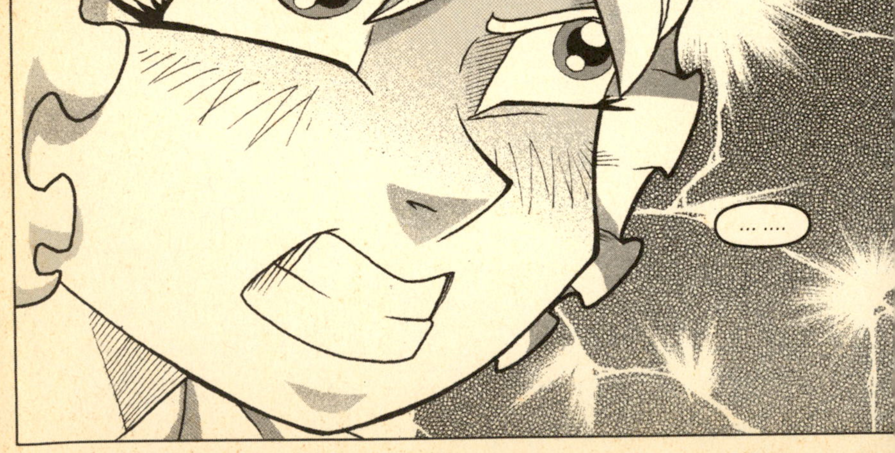
... .

YOU BIG GOON!
YOU MONSTER!!! I LOST MY FATHER!!! AND YOU ARE BEING INCREDIBLY INSENSITIVE!!!
HOW DARE YOU TREAT HIM LIKE THAT!!!
I ... I ...
HE NEEDS COMPASSION, NOT RUDENESS!!!

I DIDN'T MEAN NOTHIN' BY IT...
I JEST KNEW THE GENERAL WAS EXPECTIN' US T' ATTACK THE BRIT NAVY TONIGHT, IS ALL!

WELL, MAYBE MR. BUSHNELL HERE NEEDS A LITTLE MORE TIME!
NO!

THERE IS NO MORE TIME.
SERGEANT LEE HERE MAY BE A LITTLE ROUGH AROUND THE EDGES, MISS TEMPLETON, BUT HE IS RIGHT ABOUT ONE THING.

MY BROTHER AND I CREATED THE TURTLE BECAUSE WE WERE, AH, TRYING TO FIND A WAY TO STOP THIS WAR MORE ... MORE QUICKLY.
MY BROTHER MAY BE GONE, BUT THE WAR ISN'T.
WITH THIS WEAPON IN OUR HANDS, WE CAN STRIKE THE BRITISH FLEET WHEN THEY LEAST EXPECT IT.
WHO KNOWS ... MAYBE MY INVENTION WILL PUT AN END TO THE WAR.
I INTEND TO TRY AND KEEP TRYING.
AND THIS MAN HAS BEEN TRAINED TO USE MY WAR MACHINE.
HE AND I DON'T SEE EYE TO EYE ON MANY THINGS --
THAT'S 'CUZ YOU'RE SO SHORT.
BUT WE BOTH WANT THIS WAR OVER SOON.

IT SOUNDS LIKE THEY PLAN TO USE THE TURTLE TONIGHT.
WE NEED TO DISCUSS OFFICIAL BUSINESS.
THANK YOU FOR COMING, MISS TEMPLETON.
I'VE GOT SOME OFFICIAL BUSINESS TO DISCUSS MYSELF ...
SHOOM!

SOMETHING STRANGE ABOUT THAT GIRL ...

LAUREL, PLEASE EXPLAIN TO ME WHAT'S GOING ON!
WORMHOLE! GLAD TO SEE YOU FINISHED FIXING N.E.X.U.S.!
WELL, THAT'S BENJAMIN FRANKLIN DOWN THERE --
-- ISN'T HE THE GREATEST? --
-- AND HE'S GETTING READY TO HELP MR. BUSHNELL ATTACK THE BRITISH FLEET TONIGHT.
YOU KNOW ANYTHING ABOUT THAT BATTLE?
NO. I NEVER HEARD OF IT.
MR. BUSHNELL SEEMS TO THINK HIS TURTLE WILL WIN THE WAR, BUT I'VE NEVER HEARD OF IT.
SO I DON'T KNOW WHAT'S GOING TO HAPPEN.
MAYBE IT WILL BE DESTROYED ...

WE CAN'T WORRY ABOUT THE TURTLE.
WE MUST KEEP WATCH ON BENJAMIN FRANKLIN, SINCE HE'S DARCHON'S TARGET.
~~~~~ ~ ~~~~ ~~~~~~ ~~~~!
I SURE HOPE SO, TAK. IT'D BE NICE TO FINALLY STOP DARCHON FROM TAKING ONE SCIENTIST.
OUR MISTAKE WAS NOT DUE TO ANY ONE OF US.
IN THE END, IT WAS THE TEAM THAT MADE THE MISTAKE.
... AND YOU MUST MAKE SURE NO ONE SEES YOU.
YOU'LL MAKE YOUR WAY TO THE FLAGSHIP --
-- AND ATTACH THE BOMB! I KNOW! I KNOW!
I'VE GOT IT ALL UP HERE ...
AND AS TEAM LEADER, THE MISTAKE FELL ON MY SHOULDERS.
~~~~~

CHAPTER FOUR

NOW, TO MAKE THAT POWDER KEG STICK, YOU'VE GOT TO DRILL THE ANCHOR IN DEEP --
YEAH, YEAH, YEAH ... WHEN DO I GET TO BLOW UP STUFF?
STATUS REPORT, WORMHOLE?

STILL NO SIGN OF DARCHON ...

IT MAY NOT BE JUST DARCHON WE HAVE TO WORRY ABOUT, WORMHOLE.
REMEMBER, WHEN HE TOOK MY FATHER HE ATTACKED WITH CYBORG WASPS.
THAT'S TRUE. UP UNTIL THEN, WE DIDN'T KNOW HE COULD DO THAT.
ONE IMPORTANT STRATEGY WHEN GOING UP AGAINST AN ENEMY LIKE DARCHON ...
WONDER HOW MUCH MORE WE DON'T KNOW ABOUT HIM.
MOTHER MASS, REPORT.
I'VE GOT A WHOLE LOT OF NOTHING GOING ON OVER HERE.
KNOW YOUR OPPONENT.
I WISH I KNEW THE EXTENT OF HIS POWER.
HE SAID HE HAS ALL OF YOUR POWERS.
BE CAREFUL WHAT YOU WISH FOR.

HELLO, LADIES.
BEAUTIFUL EVENING, EH?
EVERY NEW THING WE LEARNED ABOUT DARCHON JUST MADE IT FEEL LIKE WE WERE IN OVER OUR HEADS.

TAK, WORMHOLE, MOTHER MASS ...
CONVERGE ON MY LOCATION.

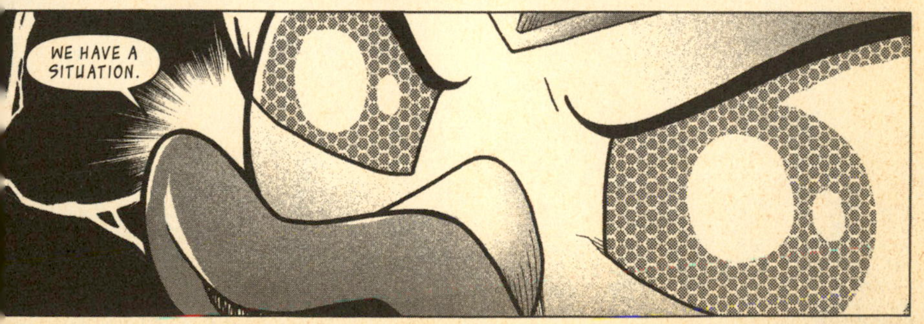
WE HAVE A SITUATION.

WHAT'S THE DATE, Wormhole ?
SEPTEMBER 7, 1776.
MARK THIS DATE DOWN, Darchon .
BECAUSE TODAY IS THE DAY YOUR MISSION OF EVIL ENDS.

FOOLISH LITTLE FLIES.
YOU FORGET, I AM YOUR SUPERIOR IN EVERY WAY, SAVE ONE.
THERE ARE *SIX* OF YOU. *ONE* OF ME.
BUT I'VE *FIXED* THAT PROBLEM.
I'VE FOUND SOME *NEW* FRIENDS.
THEY ARE A LOT LIKE *ME*, IN THAT THEY ALL HAVE ...

... A TASTE FOR FLIES!
NOW, MY PETS!
IT'S DINNERTIME!

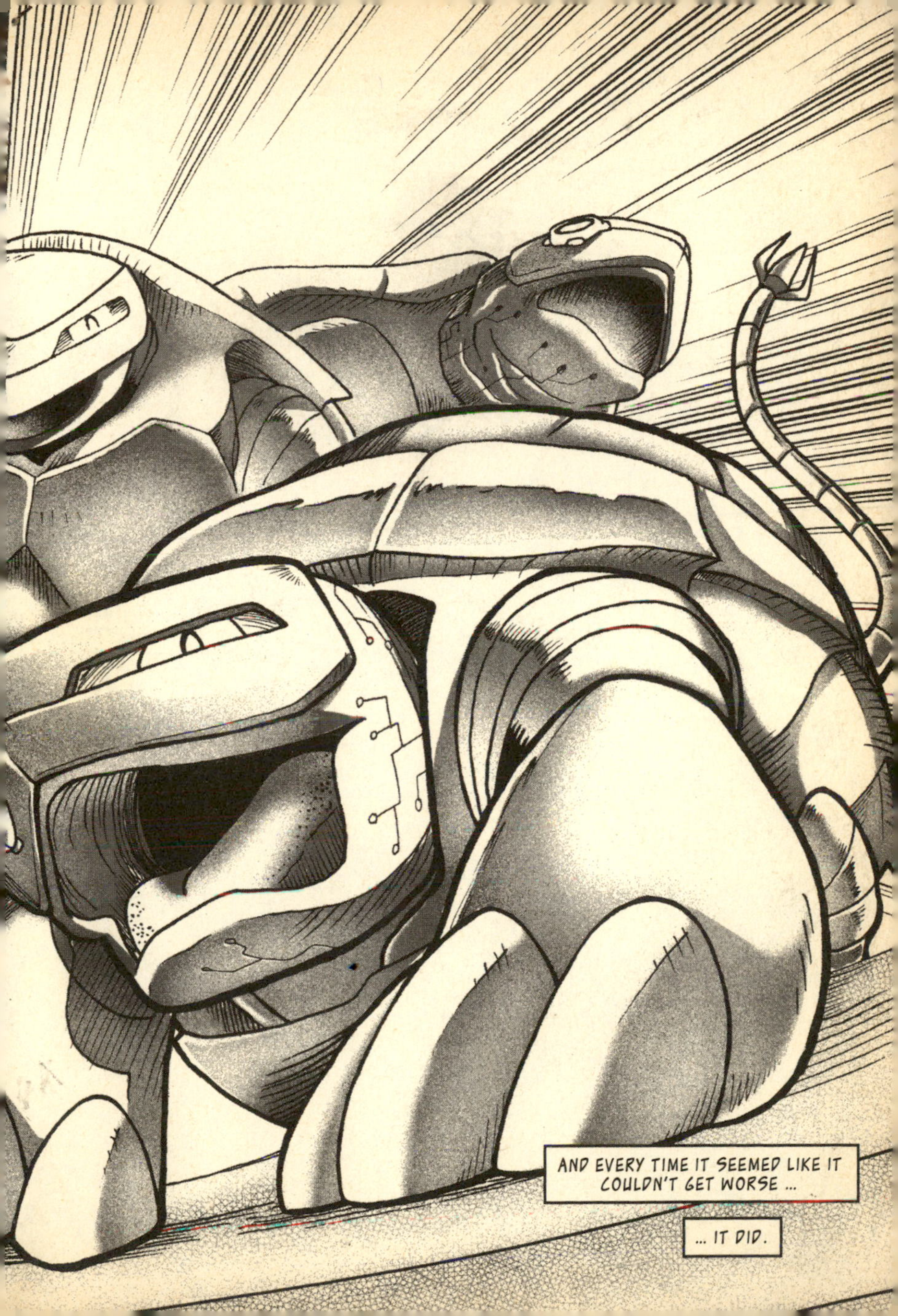
AND EVERY TIME IT SEEMED LIKE IT COULDN'T GET WORSE ...
... IT DID.

ALL RIGHT, GUYS, DRAGONFLY ATTACK PATTERN!
SLOW, LAND-BASED CREATURES COMING AFTER WINGED INSECTS?
THIS'LL BE EASIER THAN SHOOFLY PIE!

SHOOM
THEN AGAIN, I MAY HAVE SPOKEN TOO SOON.
GRAAAR!!L

FLASH!!!
WHAT DID DARCHON DO TO THOSE POOR CREATURES?!

NEVER UNDERESTIMATE ME, LITTLE FLY.
HE WAS RIGHT.

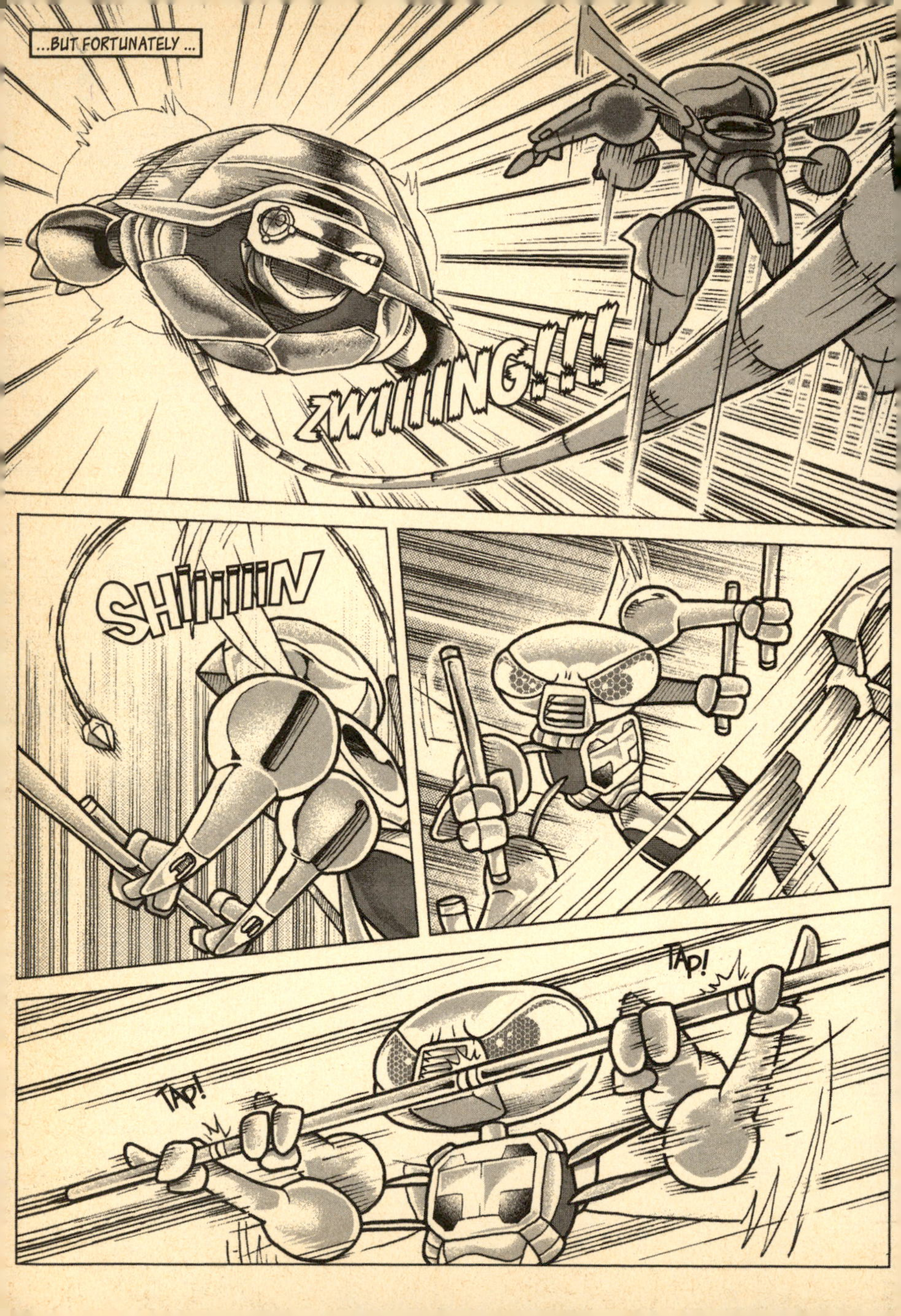
...BUT FORTUNATELY ...
ZWIIIING!!!
SHIIIIIIN
TAP!
TAP!

...I THINK ...
TRANG
CLANK!

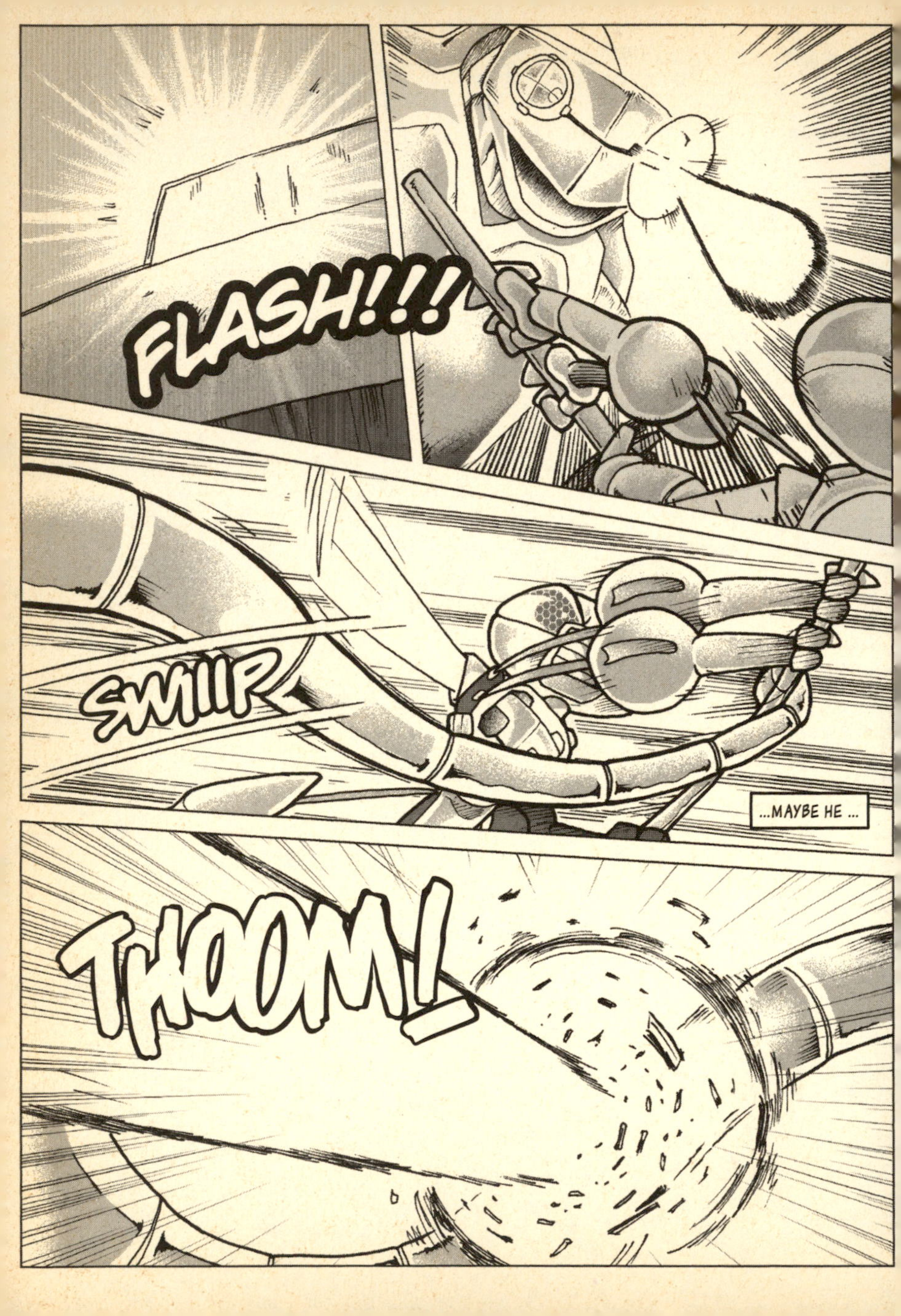
FLASH!!!
SWIIIP
...MAYBE HE ...
THOOM!

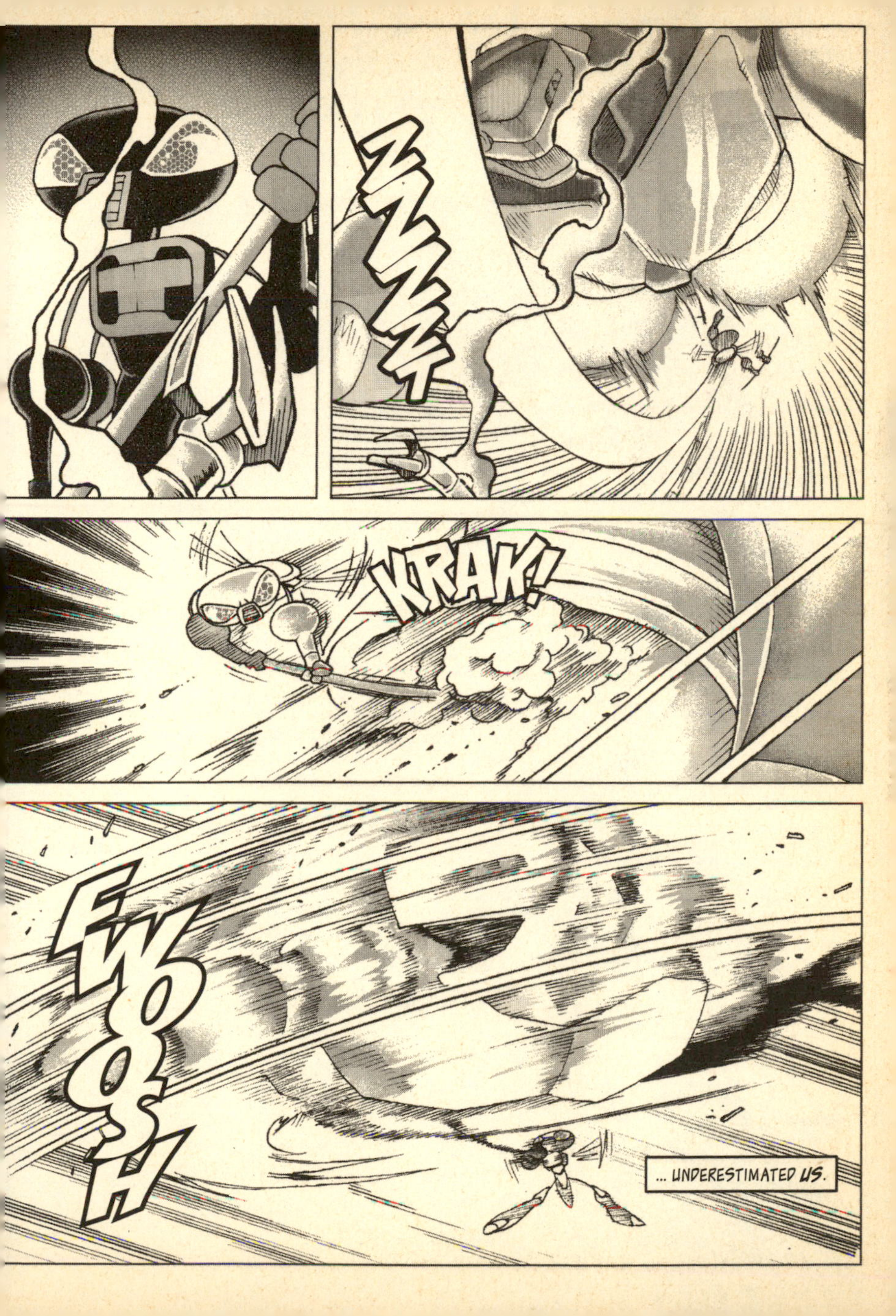
ZZZZZZZK
KRAK!
FWOOSH
... UNDERESTIMATED US.

ZWIIIIIING...!

SWOOSH!!!
OH NO YOU DON'T!
CLAP!
I AM *NOT* GOING TO BE YOUR MIDNIGHT SNACK!

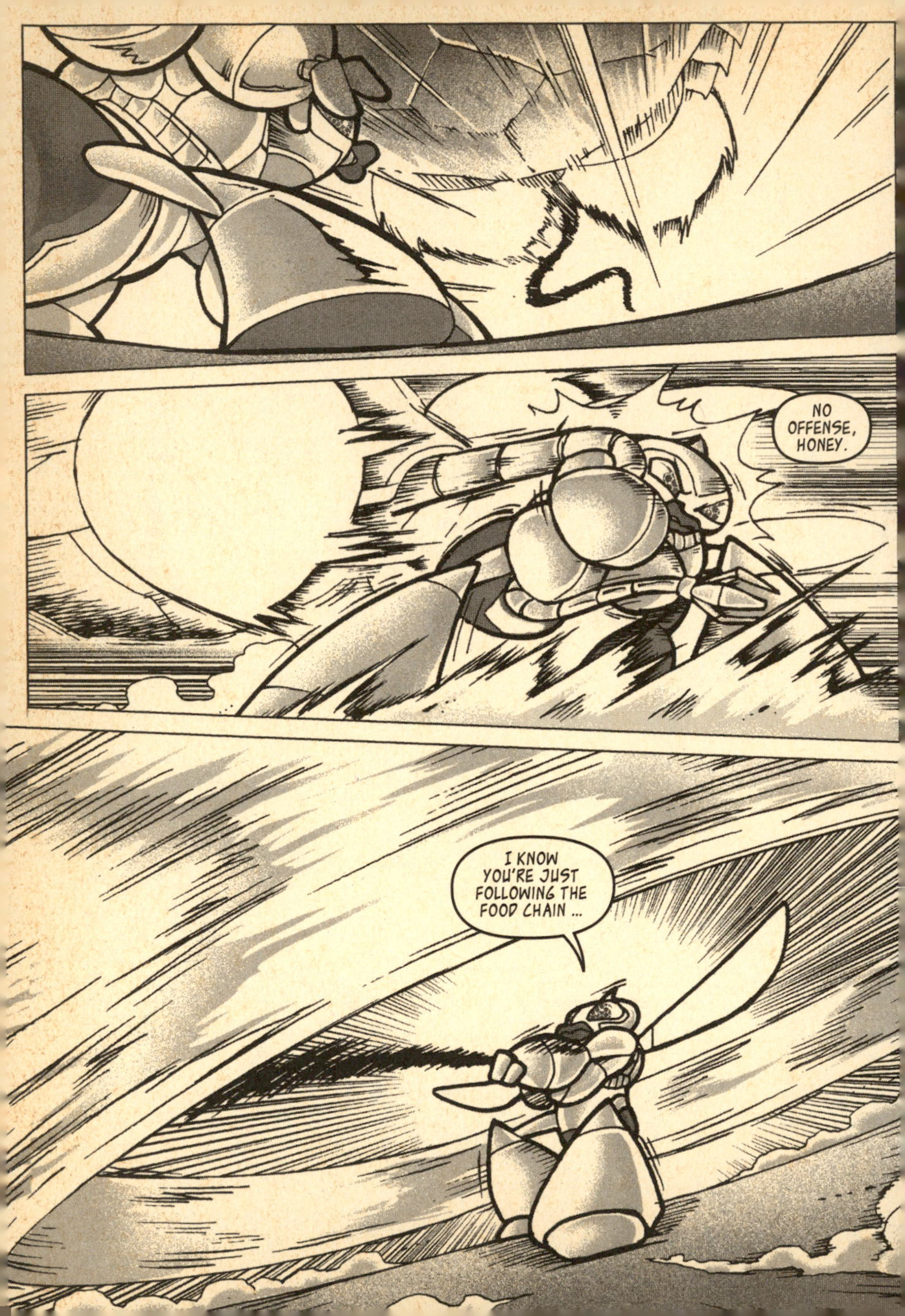
NO OFFENSE, HONEY.
I KNOW YOU'RE JUST FOLLOWING THE FOOD CHAIN ...

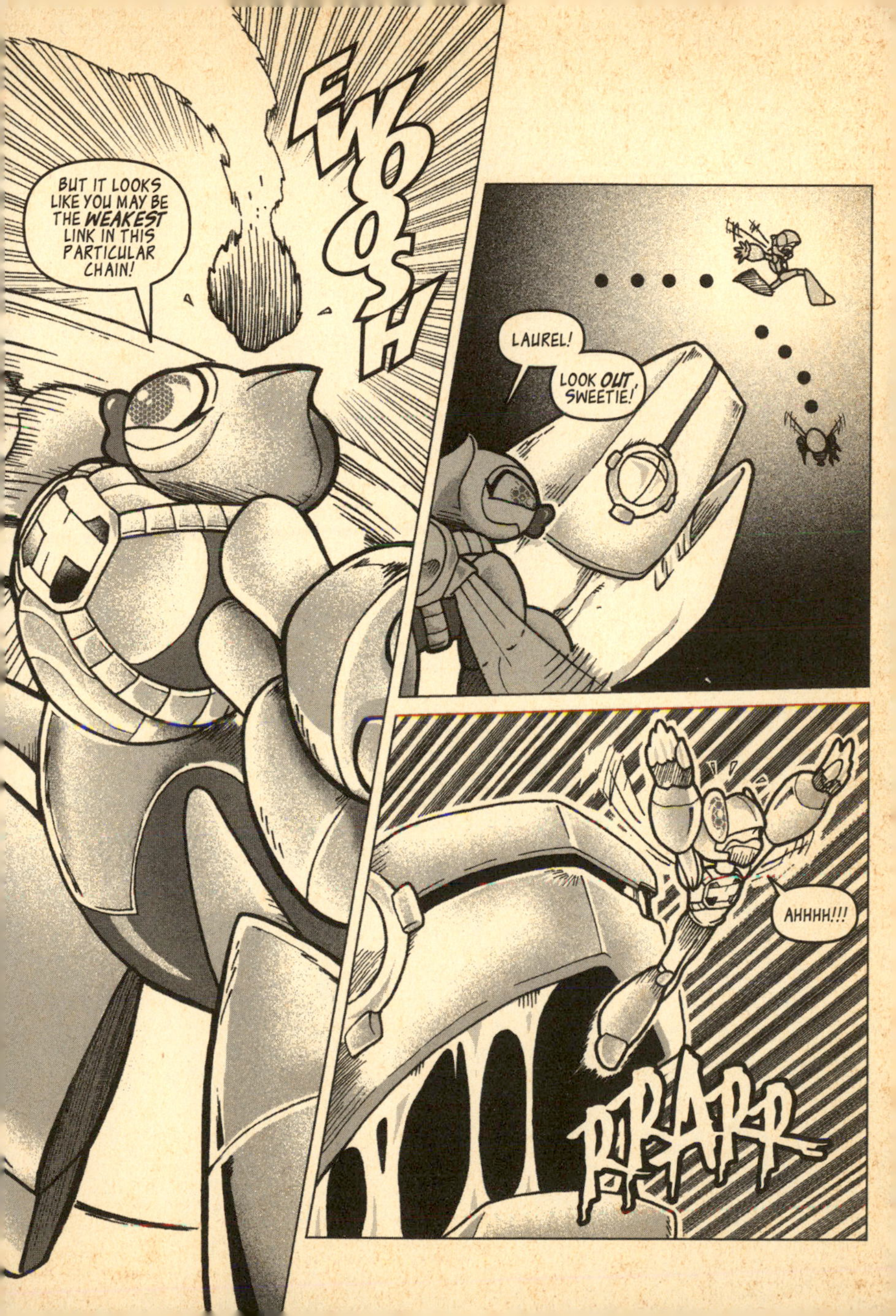
BUT IT LOOKS LIKE YOU MAY BE THE WEAKEST LINK IN THIS PARTICULAR CHAIN!
FWOOSH
LAUREL!
LOOK OUT, SWEETIE!
AHHHH!!!
RRRARR

IF IT FEELS LIKE YOU'RE ABOUT TO BE HIT BY A TON OF BRICKS, YOU'RE HALF RIGHT!
NO BRICKS ...
... JUST A TON OF MOTHER MASS!
THOOM!
OUR POWERS MAKE US A FORMIDABLE FORCE.
AND THOUGH WE'RE STILL LEARNING TEAMWORK, OUR MAIN ADVANTAGE, AS DARCHON SAID, WAS OUR NUMBERS -- OUR TEAM.

THIS IS NO GOOD.
WE'RE WASTING TOO MUCH TIME FIGHTING THESE TURTLES!
WHERE'S DARCHON!?!
HE'S NOWHERE IN SIGHT!
WE PLAYED RIGHT INTO HIS TRAP!
TAK!
WORMHOLE!
MOTHER MASS!
TAKE CARE OF THESE TURTLES!

LAUREL, BRING N.E.X.U.S. AND COME WITH ME!
WE'RE GOING TO MAKE SURE BENJAMIN FRANKLIN IS OKAY!!!
MOTHER MASS!
PLEASE DON'T HURT THOSE TURTLES!
THEY DIDN'T CHOOSE TO BE TURNED INTO FLYING FLY-EATING CYBORGS!
COME ON, N.E.X.U.S.!

YOU HEARD THE GIRL!
DON'T HURT THOSE TURTLES!
AND, UH, HOW DO YOU PROPOSE WE STOP THEM?
~~~ ~~~~ ~~~~ ~~~!
AND JUST HOW DOES "VERY GENTLY" WORK, TAK?
~~~

YOU KNOW, DON'T THINK I'M GETTIN' COLD FEET OR NOTHIN', BUT ...
... IT'S COLD DOWN THERE.
ON MY FEET.

YOU'VE PILOTED THIS BEFORE -- YOU KNOW IT LETS SOME WATER INSIDE THE BOTTOM ...
YEAH, BUT THAT WAS ALWAYS IN THE DAYTIME IN THE RIVER -- THE WATER WAS WARMER ...

LISTEN, YOU KNOW EVERYTHING YOU NEED TO KNOW.
YOU DRILL INTO THE HULL OF THE MAIN SHIP, ATTACH THE POWDER KEG, AND GET OUT OF THERE.
FAST. GOT IT?

GOT IT!
EVERYTHIN'S PUDDING!

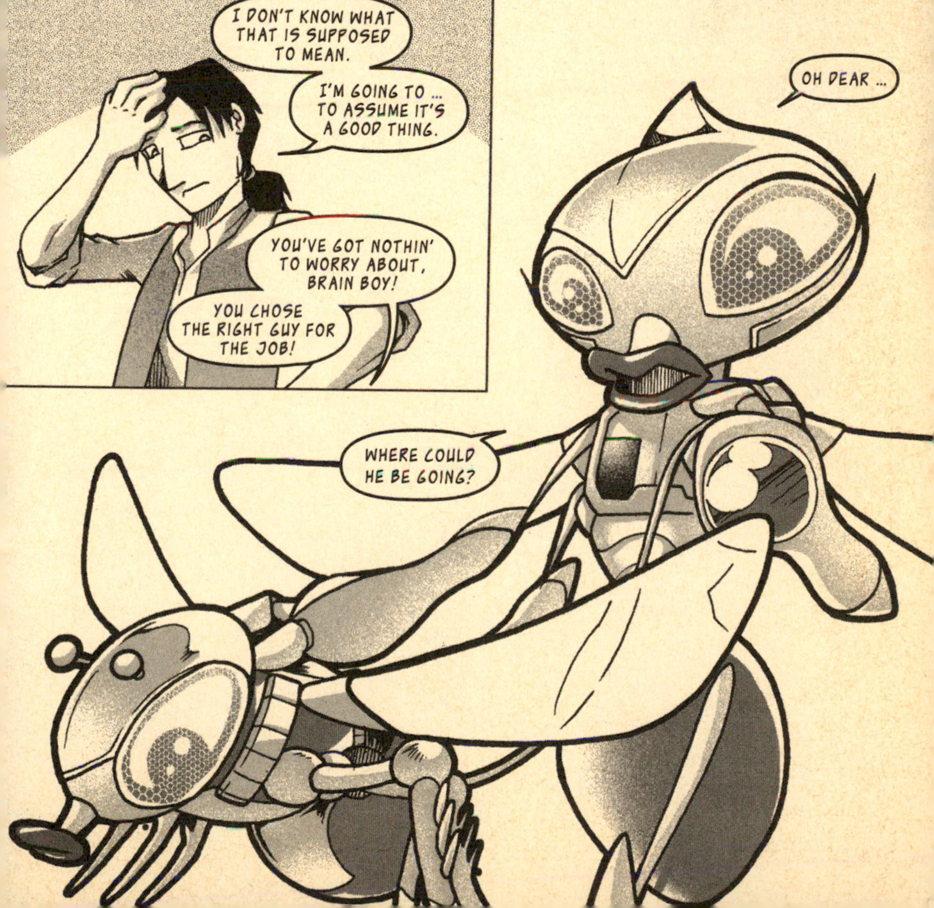
I DON'T KNOW WHAT THAT IS SUPPOSED TO MEAN.
I'M GOING TO ... TO ASSUME IT'S A GOOD THING.
YOU'VE GOT NOTHIN' TO WORRY ABOUT, BRAIN BOY!
YOU CHOSE THE RIGHT GUY FOR THE JOB!
OH DEAR ...
WHERE COULD HE BE GOING?

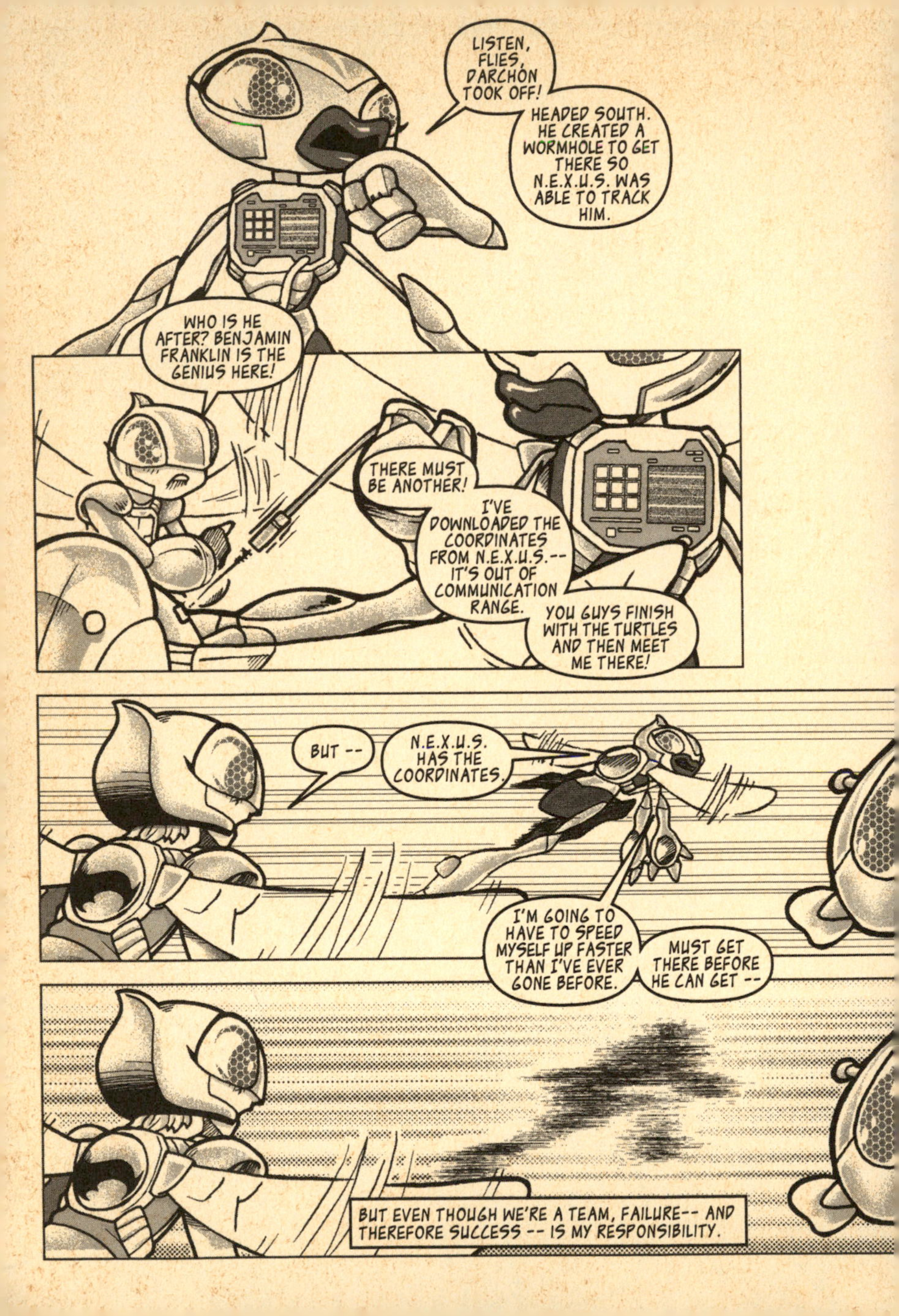
LISTEN, FLIES, DARCHON TOOK OFF!
HEADED SOUTH. HE CREATED A WORMHOLE TO GET THERE SO N.E.X.U.S. WAS ABLE TO TRACK HIM.
WHO IS HE AFTER? BENJAMIN FRANKLIN IS THE GENIUS HERE!
THERE MUST BE ANOTHER!
I'VE DOWNLOADED THE COORDINATES FROM N.E.X.U.S.-- IT'S OUT OF COMMUNICATION RANGE.
YOU GUYS FINISH WITH THE TURTLES AND THEN MEET ME THERE!
BUT --
N.E.X.U.S. HAS THE COORDINATES.
I'M GOING TO HAVE TO SPEED MYSELF UP FASTER THAN I'VE EVER GONE BEFORE.
MUST GET THERE BEFORE HE CAN GET --
BUT EVEN THOUGH WE'RE A TEAM, FAILURE-- AND THEREFORE SUCCESS -- IS MY RESPONSIBILITY.

CHAPTER FIVE
NOW, WHERE ARE YOU, DARCHON?
OUR FIRST MISTAKE: ASSUMING BENJAMIN FRANKLIN WAS THE ONLY PERSON DARCHON WOULD BE AFTER.
AND WHO ARE YOU AFTER?
IT'S THIS GUY, ISN'T IT?

I WISH LAUREL WAS HERE TO TELL ME WHO THIS GUY IS!
HELLO ...
... SLIPSTREAM.
LAUREL WAS SO STARSTRUCK BY BENJAMIN FRANKLIN ...
UH ...
INTERESTING.
WE DIDN'T EVEN THINK TO INVESTIGATE OTHER POSSIBILITIES.

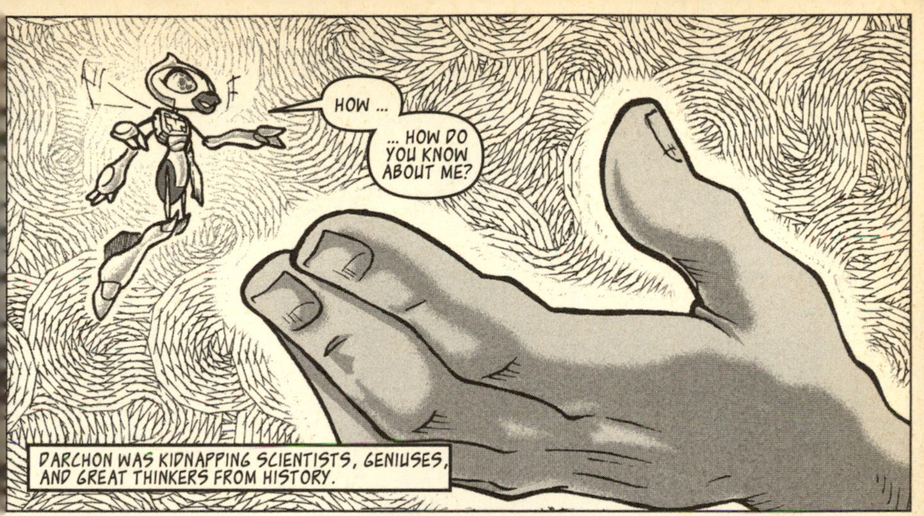
HOW ...
... HOW DO YOU KNOW ABOUT ME?
DARCHON WAS KIDNAPPING SCIENTISTS, GENIUSES, AND GREAT THINKERS FROM HISTORY.

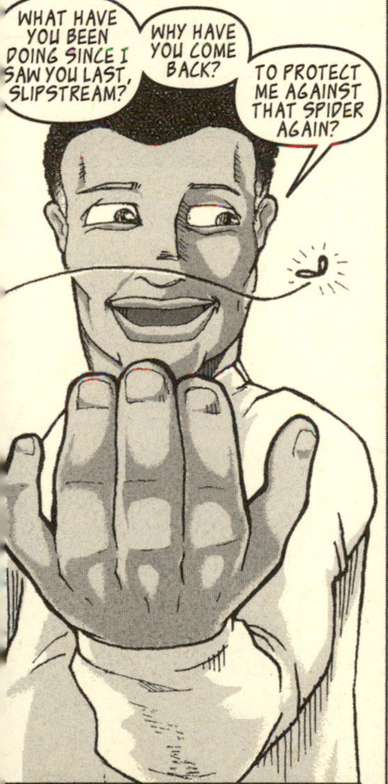
WHAT HAVE YOU BEEN DOING SINCE I SAW YOU LAST, SLIPSTREAM?
WHY HAVE YOU COME BACK?
TO PROTECT ME AGAINST THAT SPIDER AGAIN?

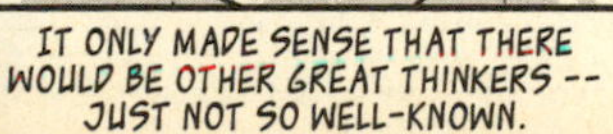
IT ONLY MADE SENSE THAT THERE WOULD BE OTHER GREAT THINKERS -- JUST NOT SO WELL-KNOWN.

"AGAIN"?

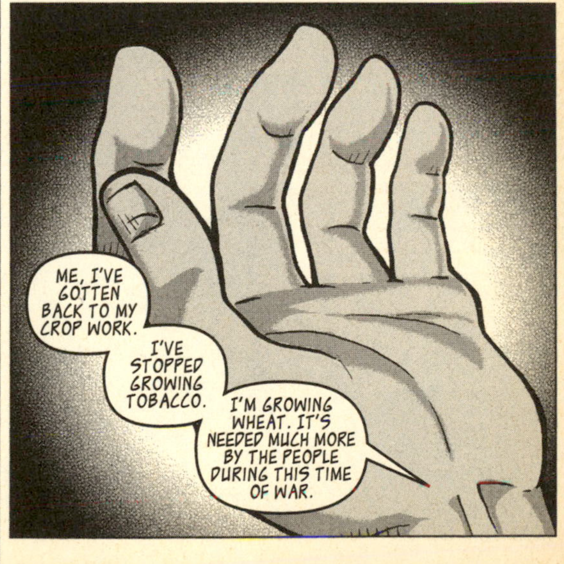
ME, I'VE GOTTEN BACK TO MY CROP WORK.
I'VE STOPPED GROWING TOBACCO.
I'M GROWING WHEAT. IT'S NEEDED MUCH MORE BY THE PEOPLE DURING THIS TIME OF WAR.

HEALTHIER TOO.
TOBACCO'S NOT GOOD FOR THE LUNGS.
IS THAT A FACT? INTERESTING.

YOU KNOW ABOUT THE WAR, DON'T YOU?
OF COURSE YOU DO.

LOOK AT THIS.
THOMAS JEFFERSON AND HIS CRONIES WROTE THIS.
IT IS REPRINTED IN ALL THE NEWSPAPERS.
THEY CALL IT THE DECLARATION OF INDEPENDENCE.

IT'S GOING TO CHANGE THE COUNTRY.
THEY ACTUALLY SAY, "ALL MEN ARE CREATED EQUAL."
YOU SEE WHAT THAT MEANS?

NO OFFENSE TO YOU AS A FLY, BUT AS A BLACK MAN IN THIS LAND, IT MEANS A WHOLE NEW WORLD IS COMING.
JUST THINK OF THE IMPLICATIONS!
AFTER THE WAR IS OVER, THINGS WILL BE SO MUCH DIFFERENT.
I APOLOGIZE. I HAVE BEEN JAWING YOUR EAR OFF --
-- DO FLIES HAVE EARS? --
-- AND I HAVEN'T GIVEN YOU THE CHANCE TO SAY MUCH.
WELL ...
YOU ALREADY KNOW ABOUT THE SPIDER?
YES. YOU TOLD ME ALL ABOUT HIM, REMEMBER?
NOT EXACTLY.
YOU SEE, I HAVEN'T MET YOU --
YOU HAVEN'T?
-- YET.

IT WOULD SEEM THAT I HAVE MET YOU BEFORE, ONLY IN YOUR PAST.
BUT YOUR PAST IS MY FUTURE ...
SO YOU HAVE NOT TRAVELED BACK INTO TIME YET TO SEE WHAT I HAVE ALREADY EXPERIENCED?

I WANTED TO SHOW YOU THIS -- TO LET YOU SEE THAT I COMPLETED IT -- BUT IT WOULD SEEM YOU WOULDN'T KNOW WHAT I AM TALKING ABOUT.

YOU MADE THIS?
SURE DID.
CARVED IT OUT OF WOOD. HAD TO USE IRON FOR THE WEIGHTS, SINCE I COULD NOT MAKE SPRINGS TO WIND WITH.
CARVED IT OUT OF WOOD?

THIS IS ... AMAZING!
A WORK OF GENIUS!
AND IT WOULD SEEM I FOUND ANOTHER POTENTIAL TARGET.

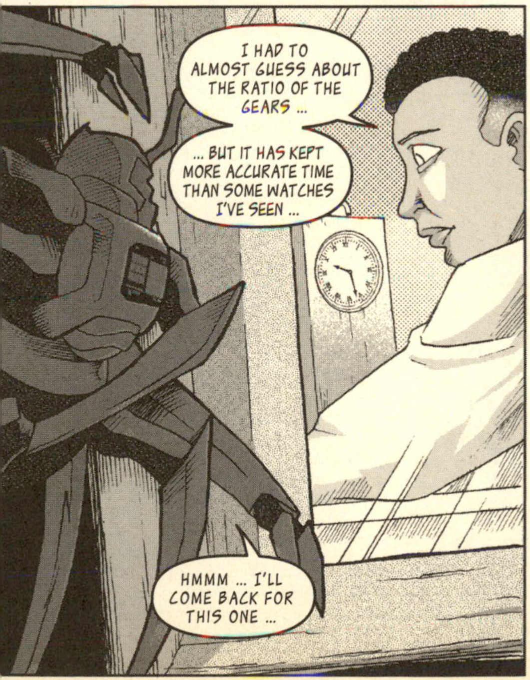
I HAD TO ALMOST GUESS ABOUT THE RATIO OF THE GEARS ...
... BUT IT HAS KEPT MORE ACCURATE TIME THAN SOME WATCHES I'VE SEEN ...
HMMM ... I'LL COME BACK FOR THIS ONE ...

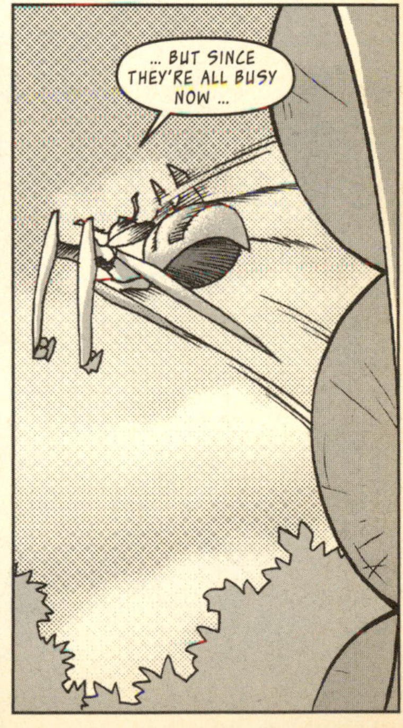
... BUT SINCE THEY'RE ALL BUSY NOW ...

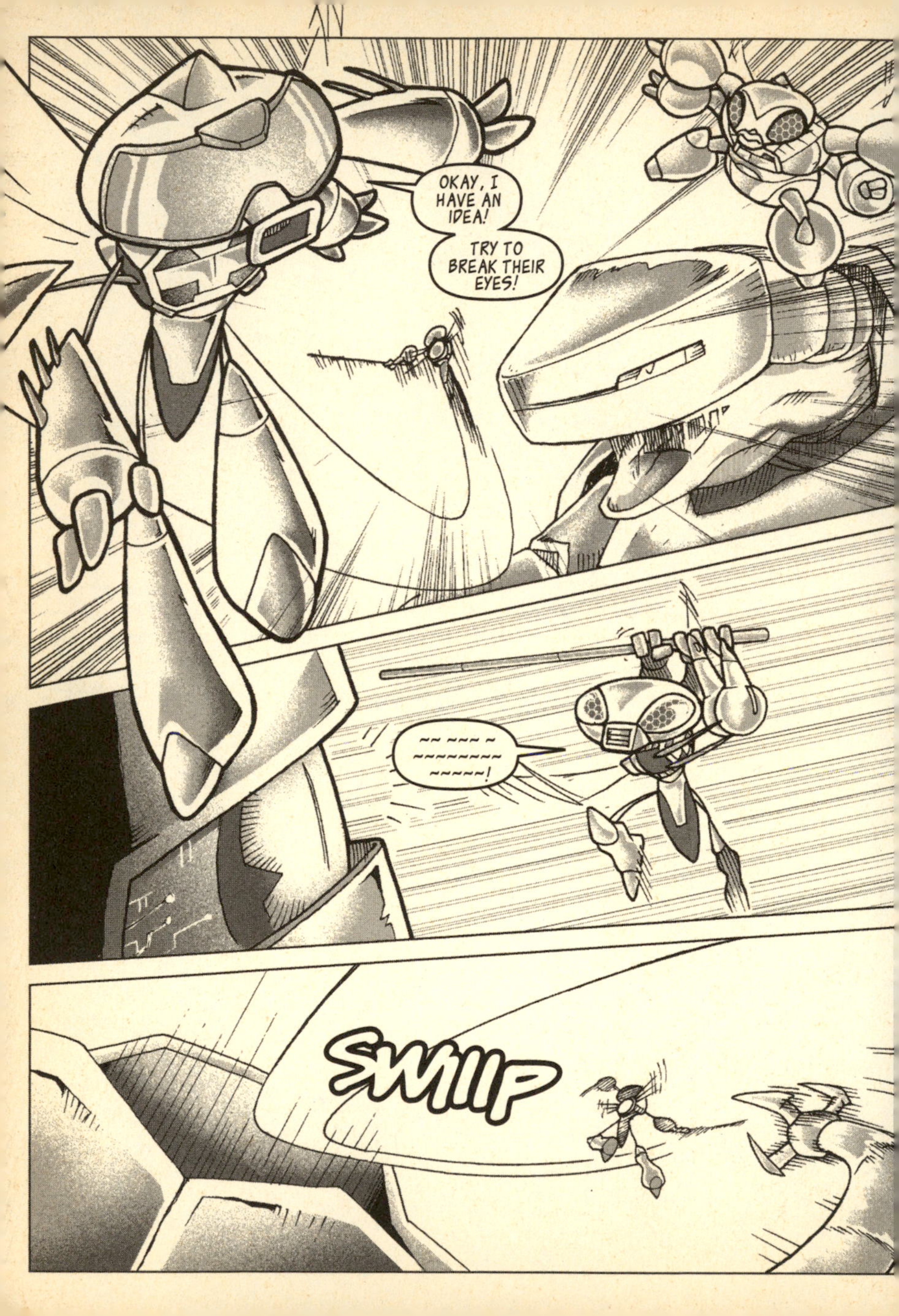
OKAY, I HAVE AN IDEA!
TRY TO BREAK THEIR EYES!
~~ ~~~ ~ ~~~~~~~~ ~~~~~!
SWIIP

SMAK
TAK HAS A GOOD POINT!
EVEN IF HE COULD HIT THEIR EYE, THAT SOUNDS LIKE SOMETHING THAT WOULD HURT THE TURTLES!
AND WE PROMISED NOT TO DO THAT!
WELL, I CAN'T THINK OF ANYTHING ELSE!
WHY'D YOU GO AND MAKE THAT PROMISE ANYWAY?!

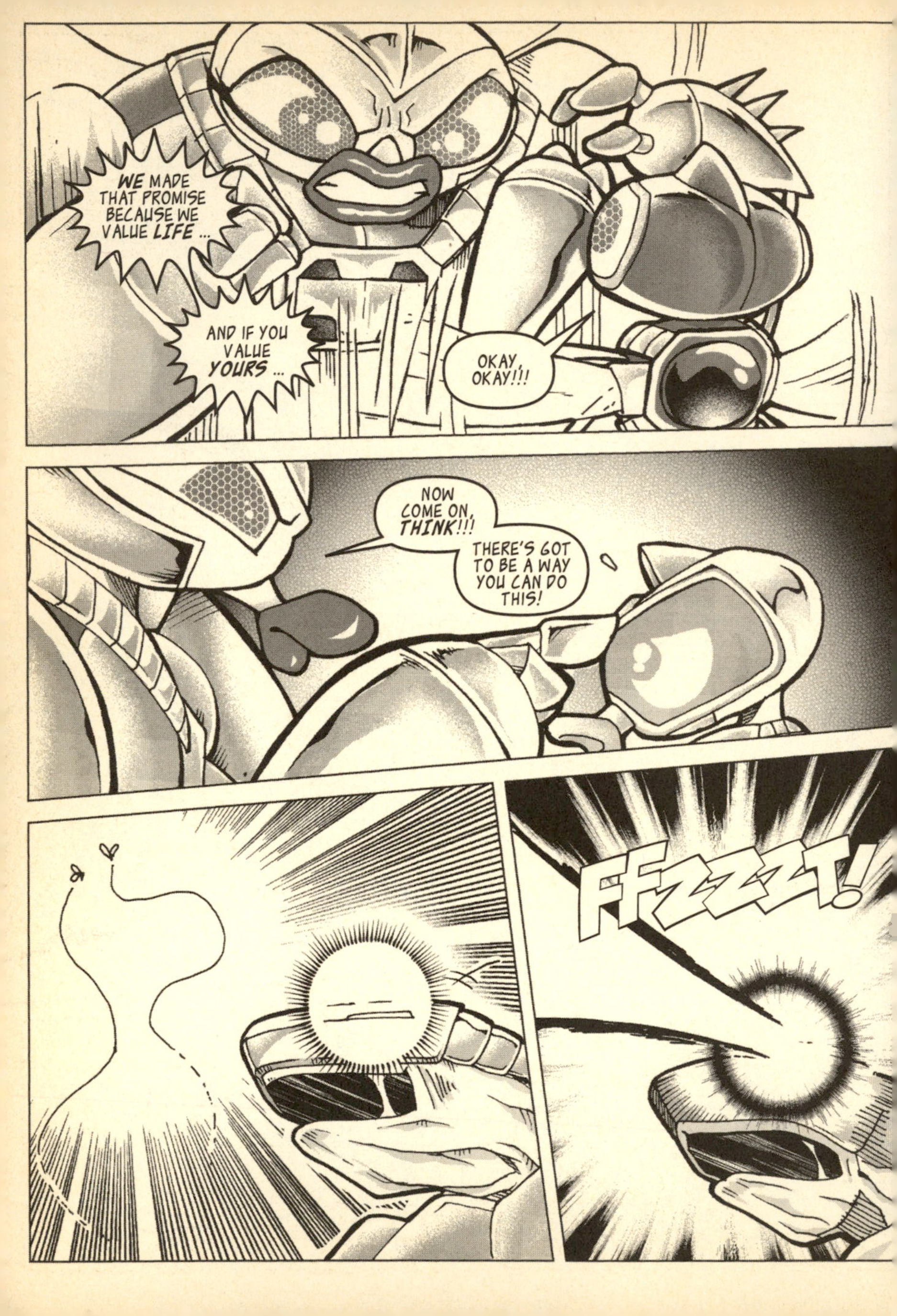
WE MADE THAT PROMISE BECAUSE WE VALUE LIFE ...
AND IF YOU VALUE YOURS ...
OKAY, OKAY!!!
NOW COME ON, THINK!!!
THERE'S GOT TO BE A WAY YOU CAN DO THIS!
FFZZZZT!

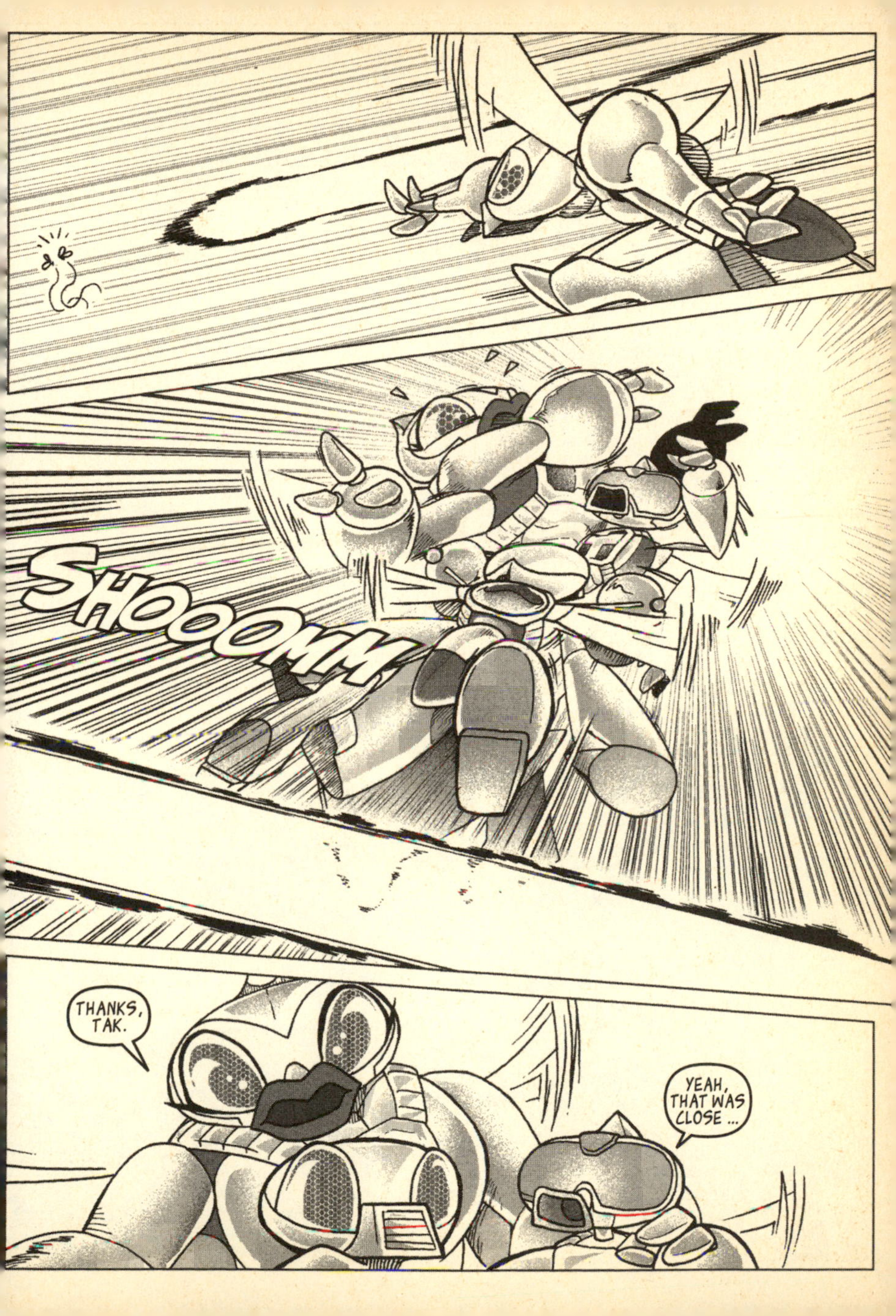
SHOOOMM
THANKS, TAK.
YEAH, THAT WAS CLOSE ...

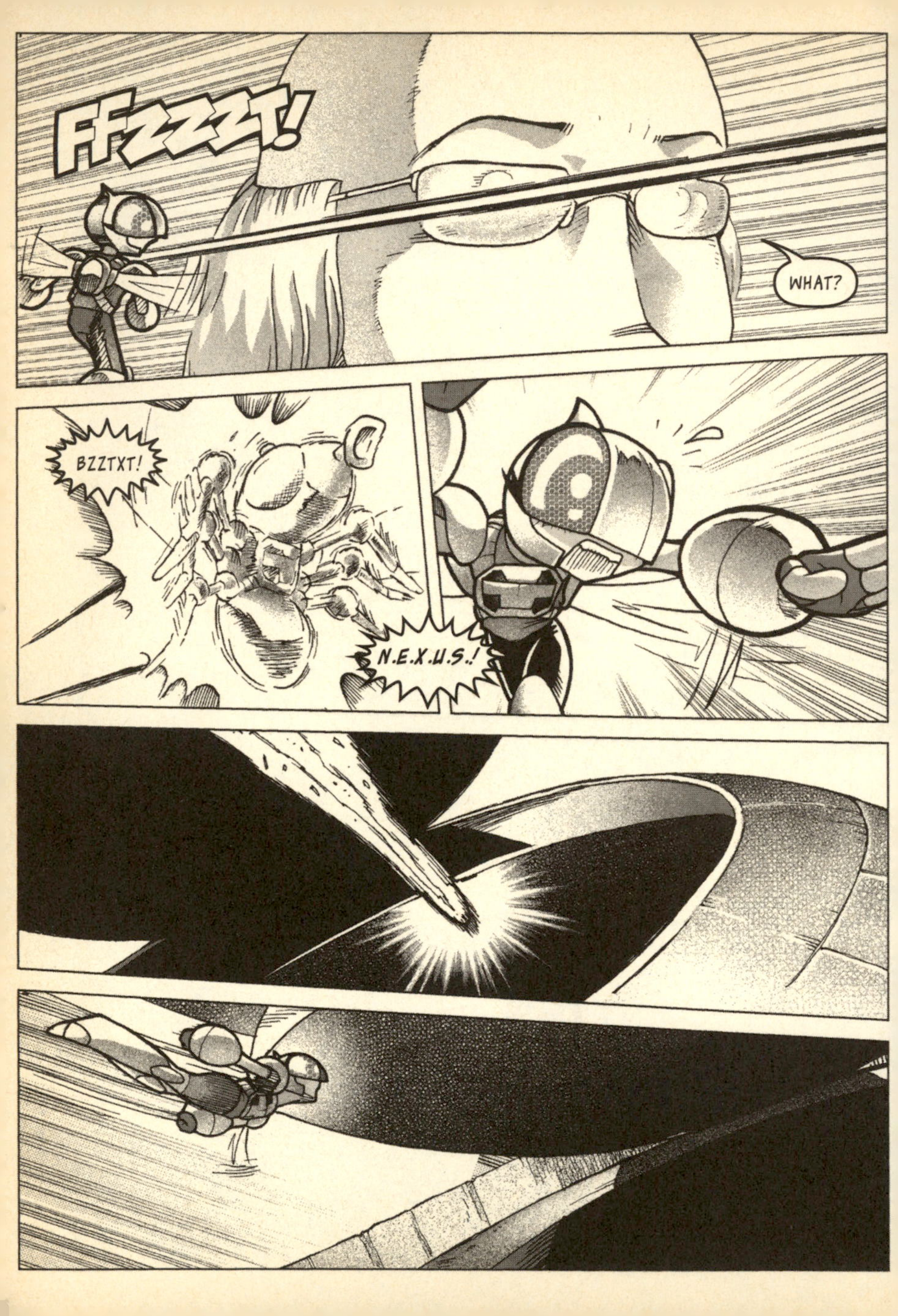
FFZZZZT!
WHAT?
BZZTXT!
N.E.X.U.S.!

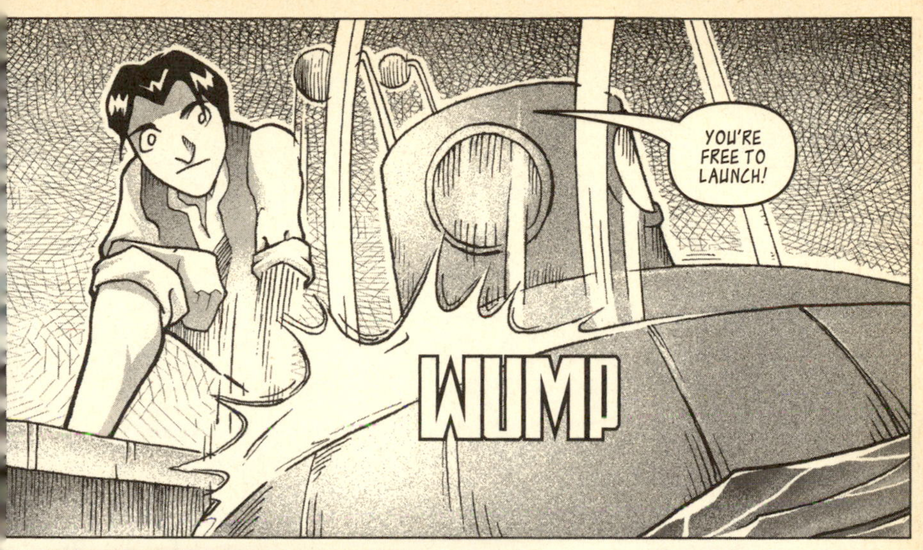
YOU'RE FREE TO LAUNCH!
WUMP

"FREE TO LAUNCH"?

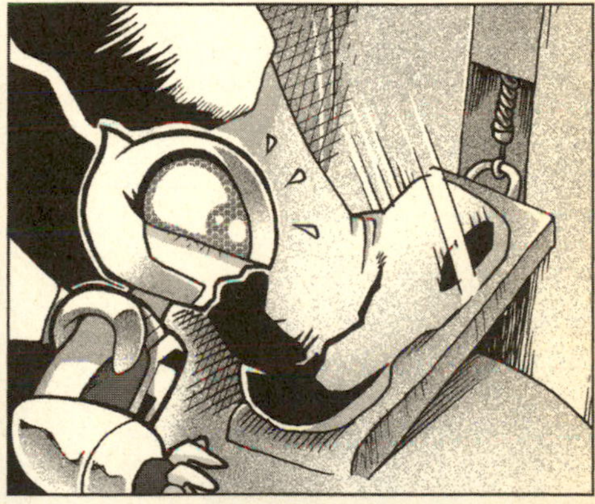

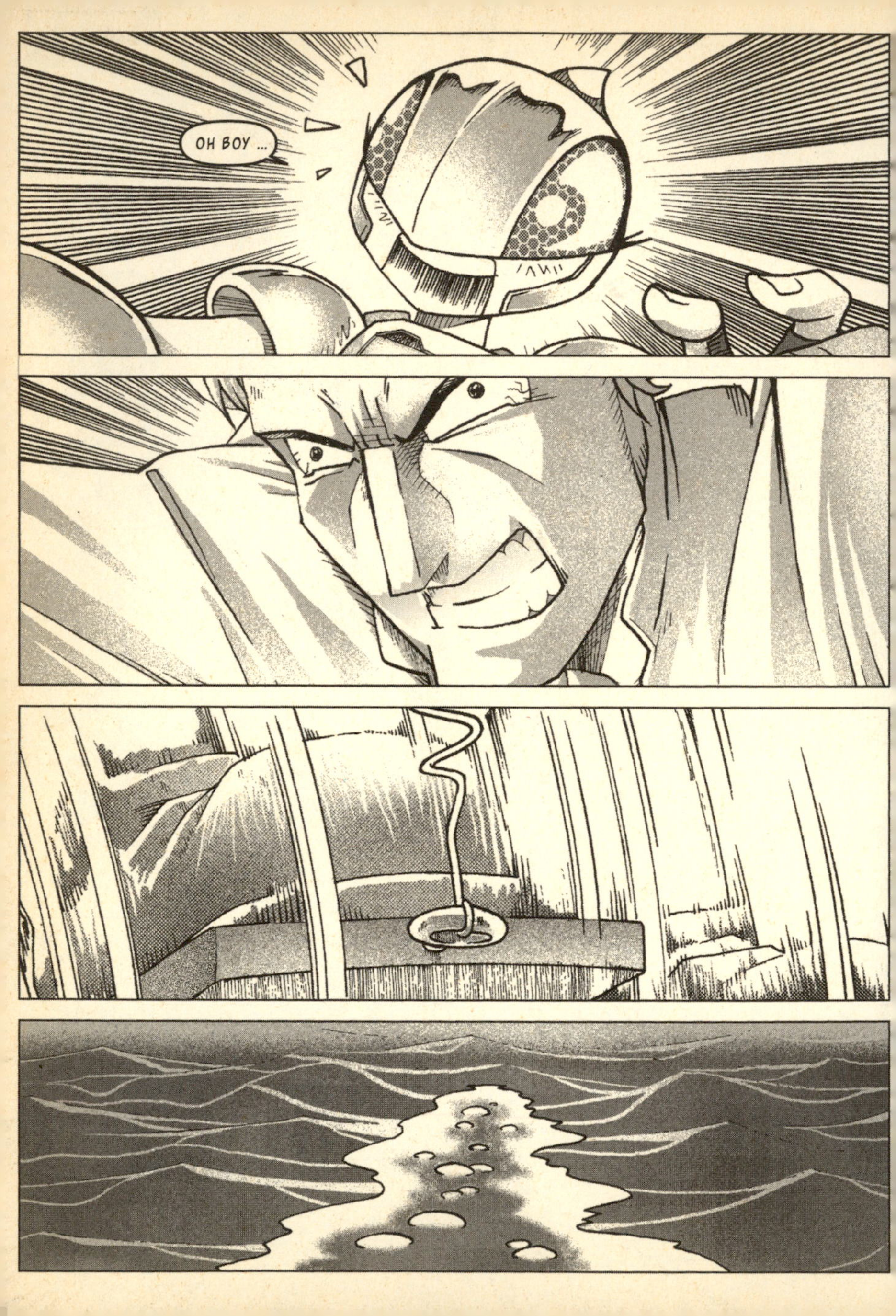
OH BOY ...

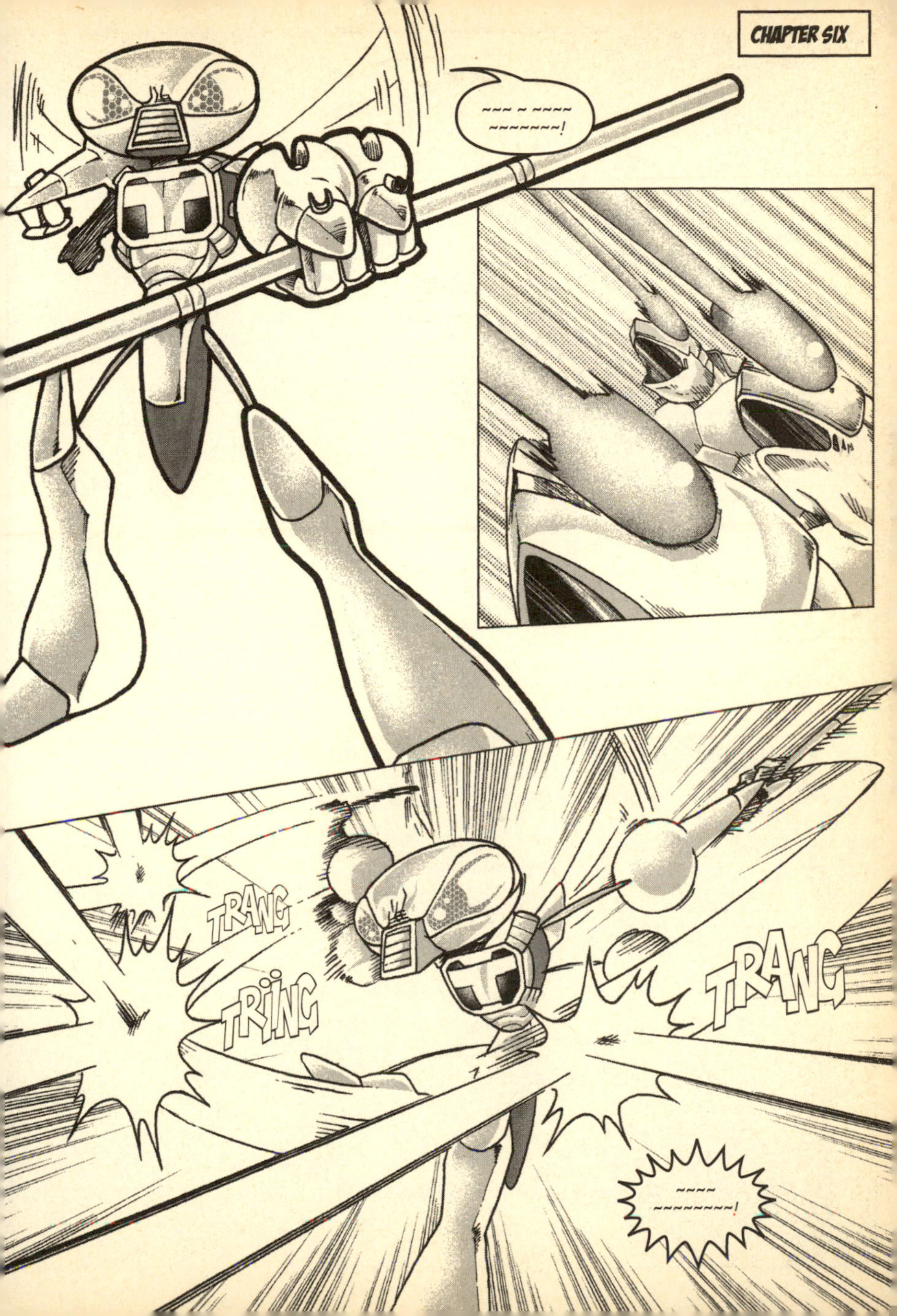
TRANG
TRING
TRANG

I'VE **GOT** IT!

WHAT IF I CREATED A WORMHOLE AND **SPLIT** THE END IN TWO ...
... SO THAT OUT **ONE** END ONLY BIOLOGICAL MATTER WOULD COME THROUGH ...
... AND OUT THE **OTHER** END, SYNTHETIC MATERIAL!

I HAVE NO IDEA WHAT YOU JUST SAID.
I THINK I CAN SEPARATE THE **LIVING** PARTS OF THE TURTLES FROM THE ROBOT PARTS!
THAT, I UNDERSTAND.

TAK!
I'M GOING TO CREATE A WORMHOLE HERE!
YOU AND MOTHER MASS NEED TO GET THE **TURTLES** TO COME THROUGH!

AW, MAN, WORMHOLE IS NOT GOING TO BE HAPPY.
HE JUST FIXED YOU!

I SURE HOPE YOU STILL WORK ...

AW, THAT IS JUST WONDERFUL!
A DIRTY, NO-GOOD FLY IS STUCK IN HERE WITH ME!

HEY, WATCH IT, YOU BIG BULLY!

WHO SAID THAT?!

ME!
MISS ... MISS TEMPLETON?
HOW'D YOU GET SO SMALL?
IT'S A LONG STORY.
NOW, CAN YOU PLEASE TURN THIS AROUND AND ...
NO WAY, NO HOW, LITTLE LADY!
ARE YOU SOME KIND OF FAIRY-ELF THING?
NO, I'M A GIRL ... JUST SMALLER THAN MOST.
NOW, PLEASE, I NEED YOU TO TURN THIS THING AROUND!
CAN'T ... I'VE GOT A JOB TO DO!

SEE?
I GOT ME SOME BRITISH NAVY SHIPS TO GET BLOWED UP!

AND DOWN WE GO ...

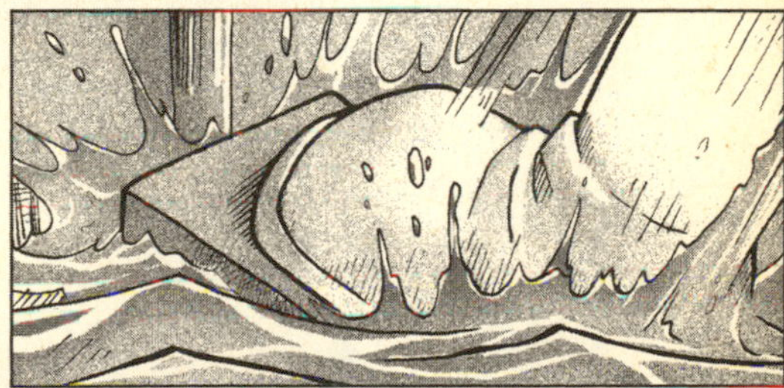

NOW, I JUST HAVE TO DRIVE THIS SCREW INTO THE BOTTOM OF THE BOAT, DROP THE BOMB, AND WE'LL HEAD BACK.
THAT'S ALL?

THAT'S ALL!

THIS'LL SHOW THEM BRITISH THAT THEY AIN'T BETTER THAN US!

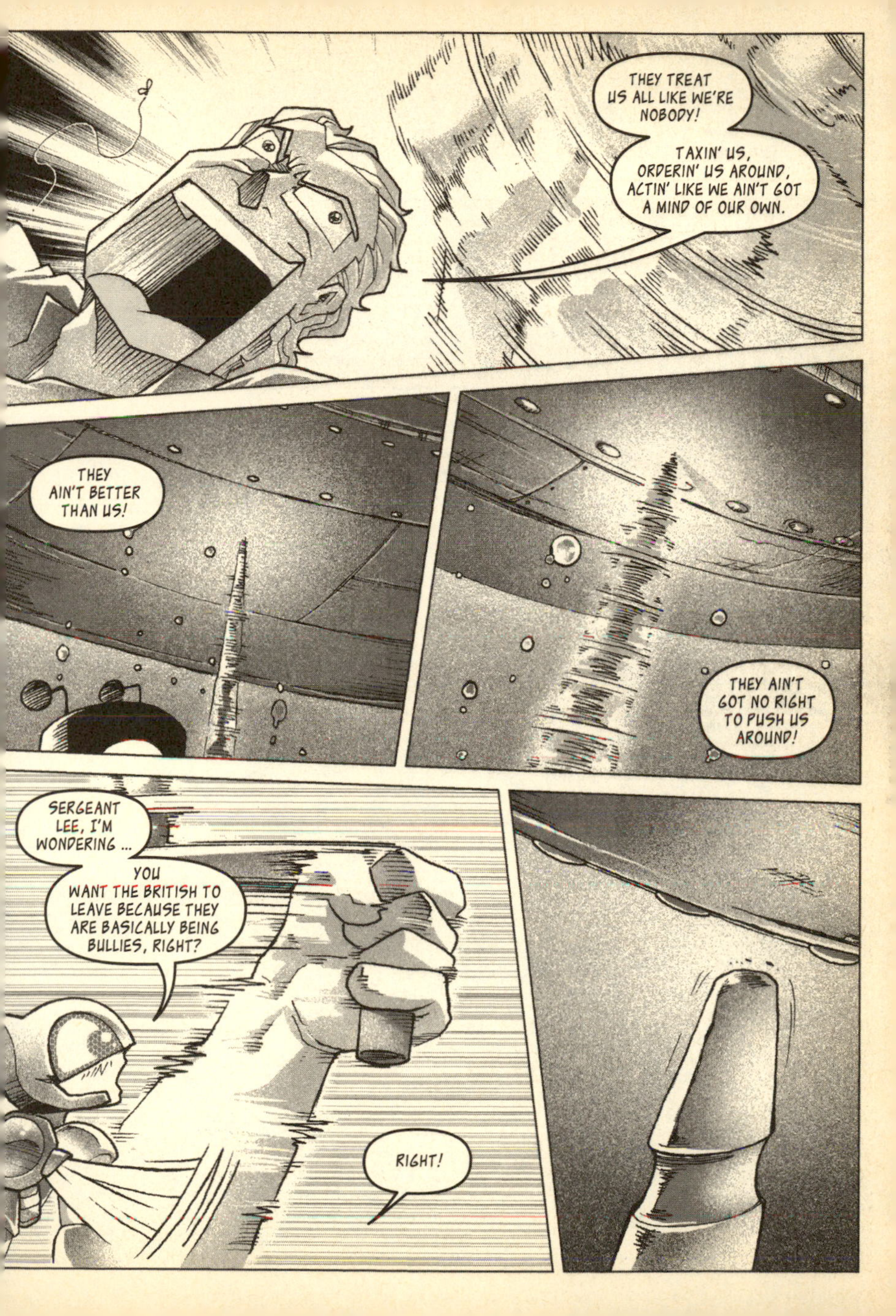
THEY TREAT US ALL LIKE WE'RE NOBODY!
TAXIN' US, ORDERIN' US AROUND, ACTIN' LIKE WE AIN'T GOT A MIND OF OUR OWN.
THEY AIN'T BETTER THAN US!
THEY AIN'T GOT NO RIGHT TO PUSH US AROUND!
SERGEANT LEE, I'M WONDERING ...
YOU WANT THE BRITISH TO LEAVE BECAUSE THEY ARE BASICALLY BEING BULLIES, RIGHT?
RIGHT!

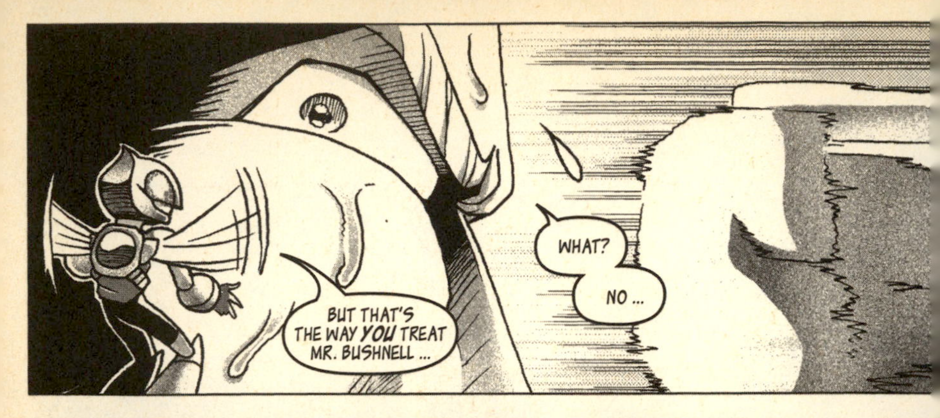

BUT THAT'S THE WAY *YOU* TREAT MR. BUSHNELL ...
WHAT?
NO ...

THIS AIN'T WORKIN'!
GONNA TRY A LITTLE HIGHER.

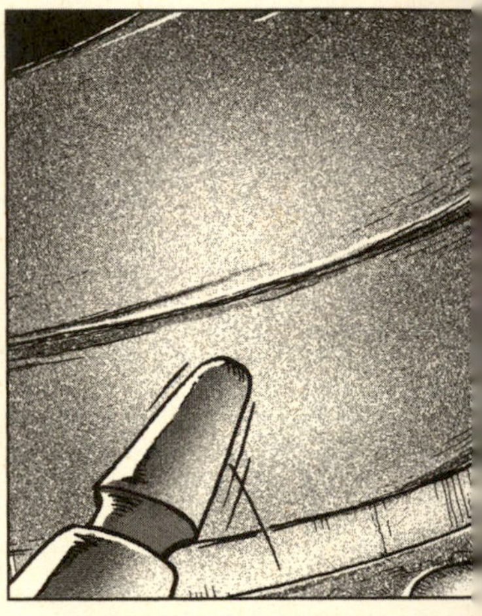

I MEAN, I'M JUST DOIN' THAT 'CAUSE SOME PEOPLE *IS* BETTER THAN OTHER PEOPLE.
I MEAN, LOOK AT THAT EGG-HEADED BIRDBRAIN!

HE COULDN'T DO THIS WITHOUT MY MUSCLE!

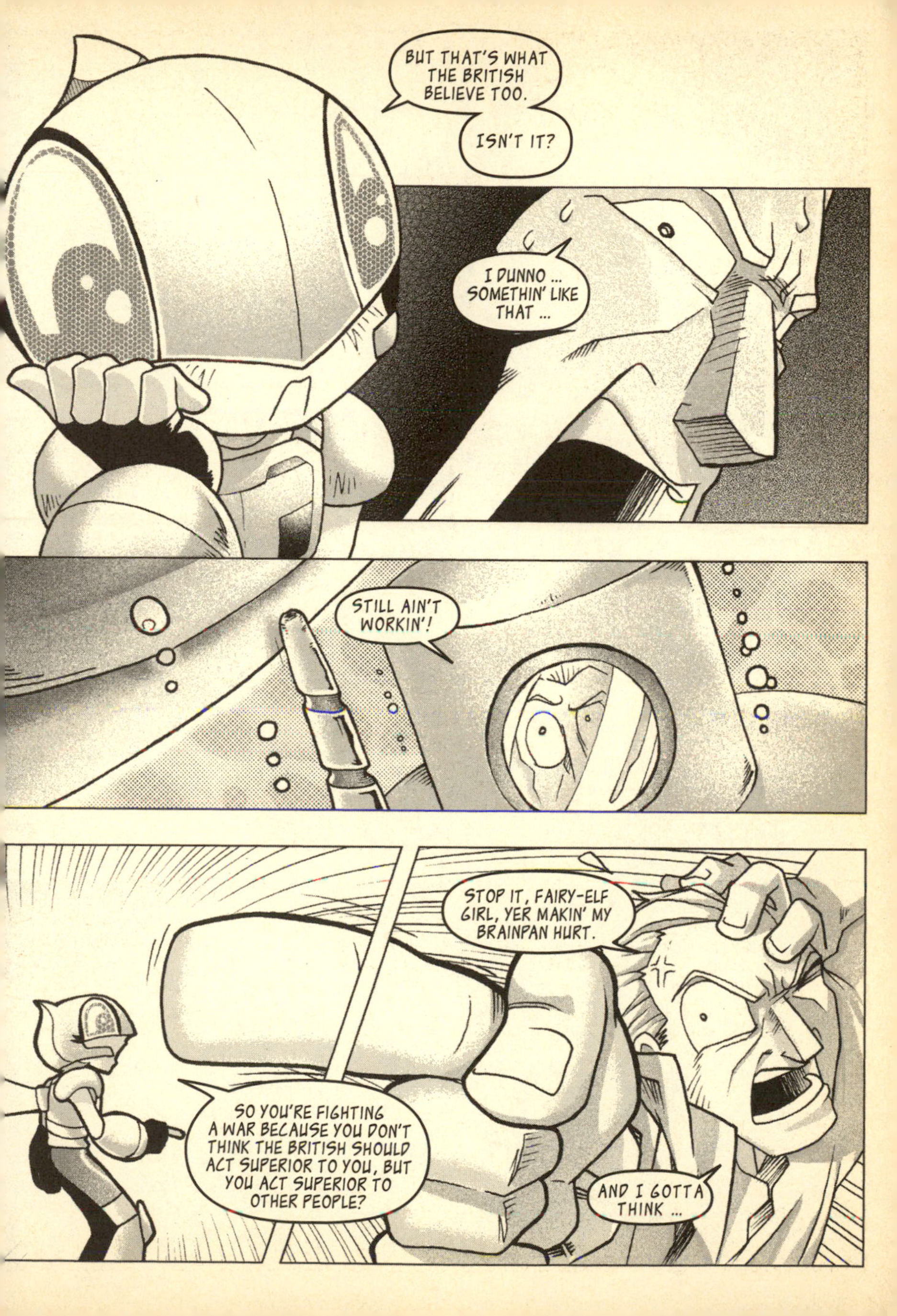
BUT THAT'S WHAT THE BRITISH BELIEVE TOO.
ISN'T IT?
I DUNNO ... SOMETHIN' LIKE THAT ...
STILL AIN'T WORKIN'!
STOP IT, FAIRY-ELF GIRL, YER MAKIN' MY BRAINPAN HURT.
SO YOU'RE FIGHTING A WAR BECAUSE YOU DON'T THINK THE BRITISH SHOULD ACT SUPERIOR TO YOU, BUT YOU ACT SUPERIOR TO OTHER PEOPLE?
AND I GOTTA THINK ...

KLIK
CLANK!
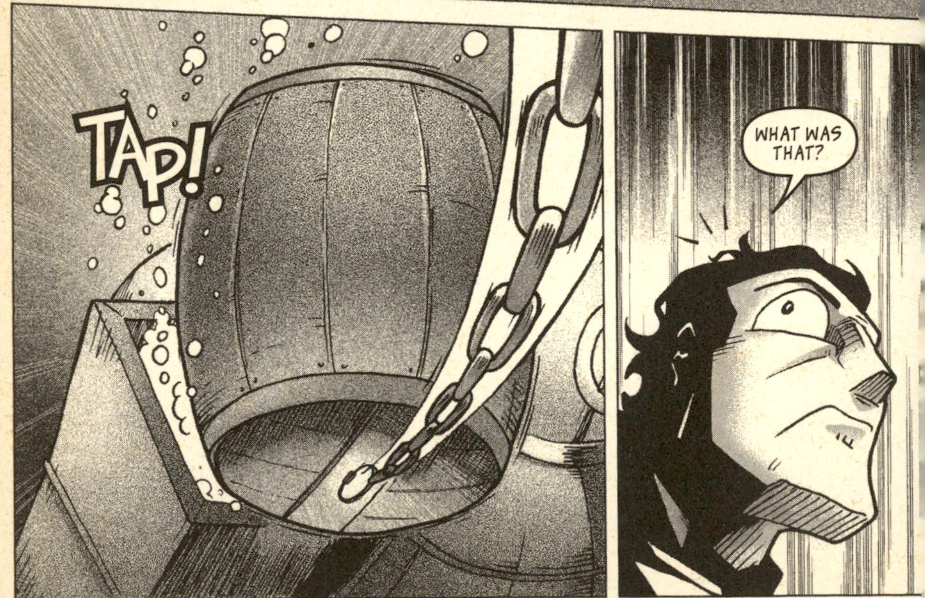
TAP!
WHAT WAS THAT?

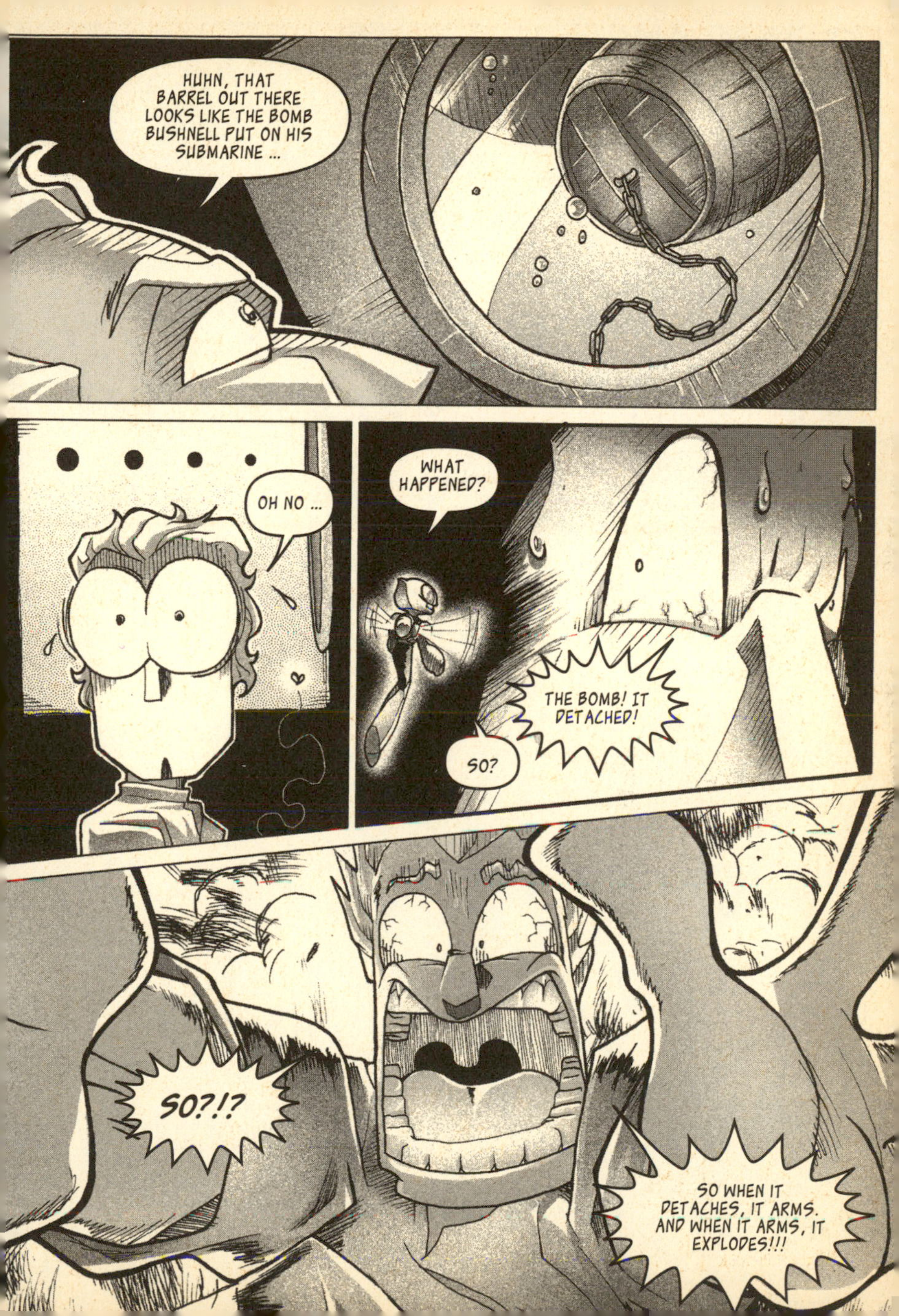
HUHN, THAT BARREL OUT THERE LOOKS LIKE THE BOMB BUSHNELL PUT ON HIS SUBMARINE ...
• • • •
OH NO ...
WHAT HAPPENED?
THE BOMB! IT DETACHED!
SO?
SO?!?
SO WHEN IT DETACHES, IT ARMS. AND WHEN IT ARMS, IT EXPLODES!!!

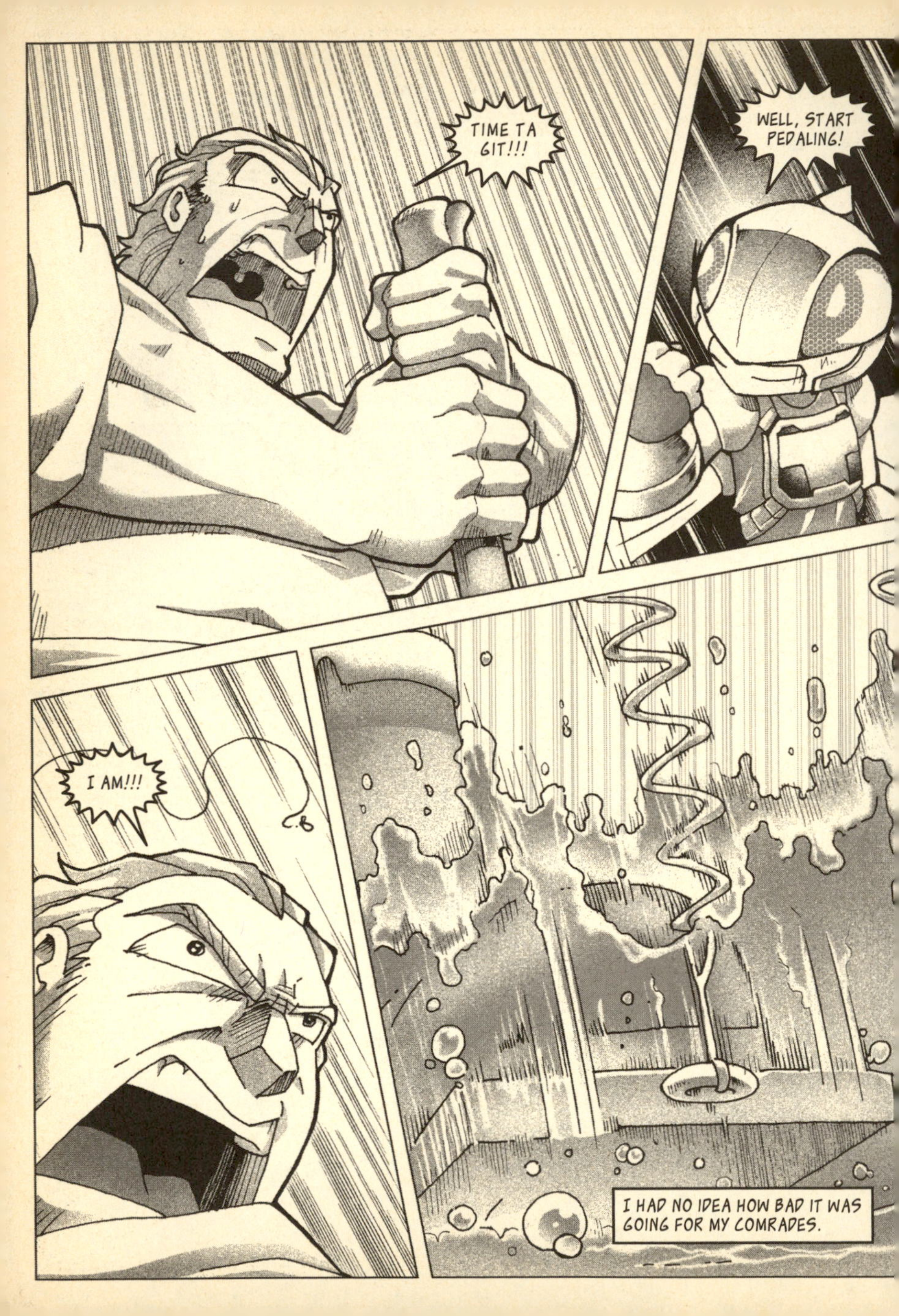
TIME TA GIT!!!
WELL, START PEDALING!
I AM!!!
I HAD NO IDEA HOW BAD IT WAS GOING FOR MY COMRADES.

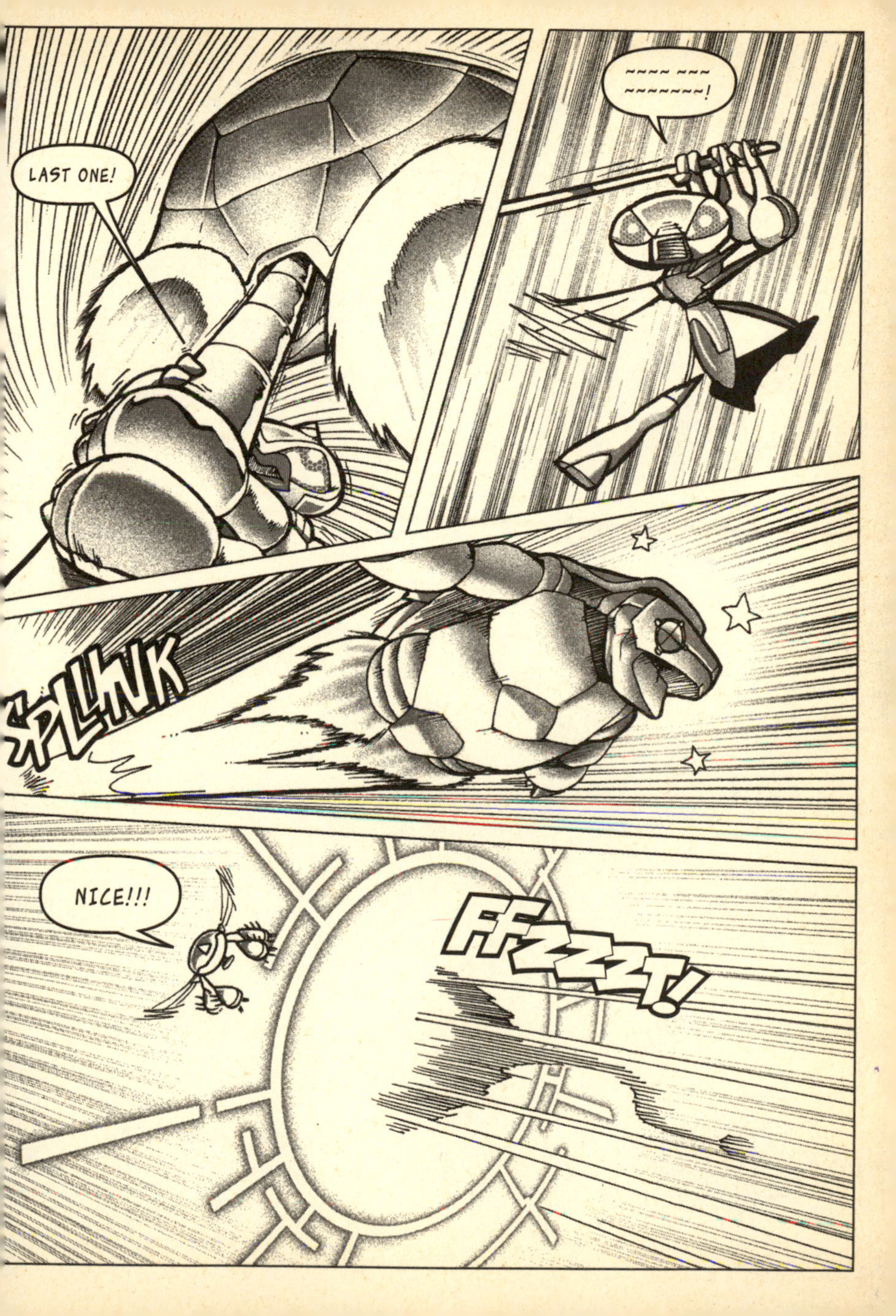
LAST ONE!
SPLINK
NICE!!!
FFZZZT!

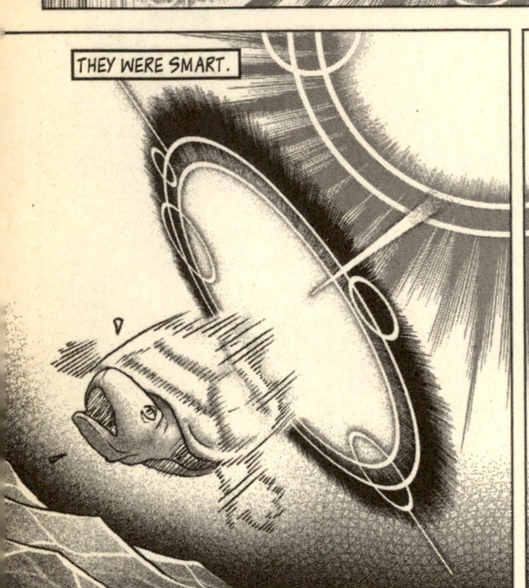
THEY WERE SMART.

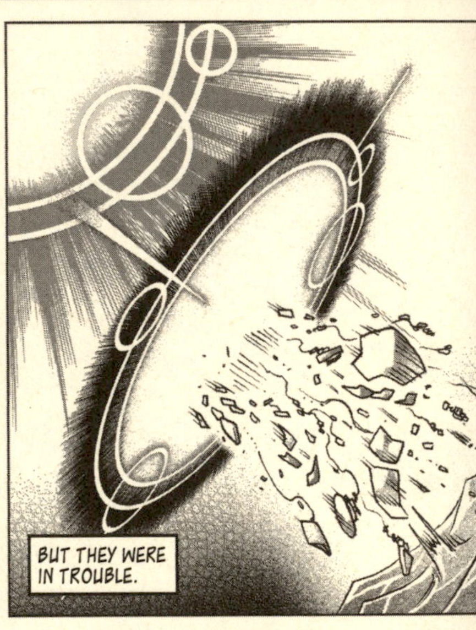
BUT THEY WERE IN TROUBLE.

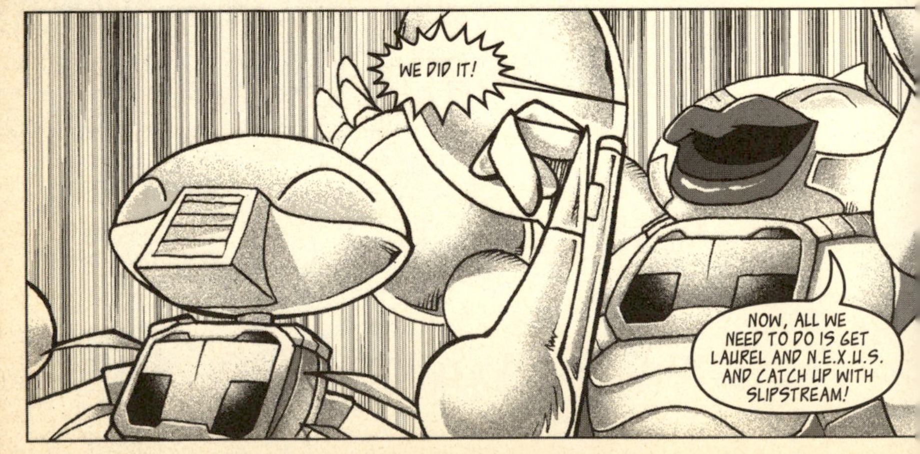
WE DID IT!
NOW, ALL WE NEED TO DO IS GET LAUREL AND N.E.X.U.S. AND CATCH UP WITH SLIPSTREAM!

YEAH ... THAT'S ALL WE NEED TO DO ...
WHERE ARE THEY?

UH, IF I HAD N.E.X.U.S. WITH ME, I COULD SCAN FOR THEM ...
BUT THAT WON'T, UH, EXACTLY WORK, YOU KNOW, WITHOUT ...
IF ONLY WE HAD SOME SORT OF SIGN TELLING US WHERE THEY MIGHT BE ...

KABLOOMM!!!
BIG TROUBLE.

IT WORKED!
MY BOY, WELL DONE! YOU DID IT!

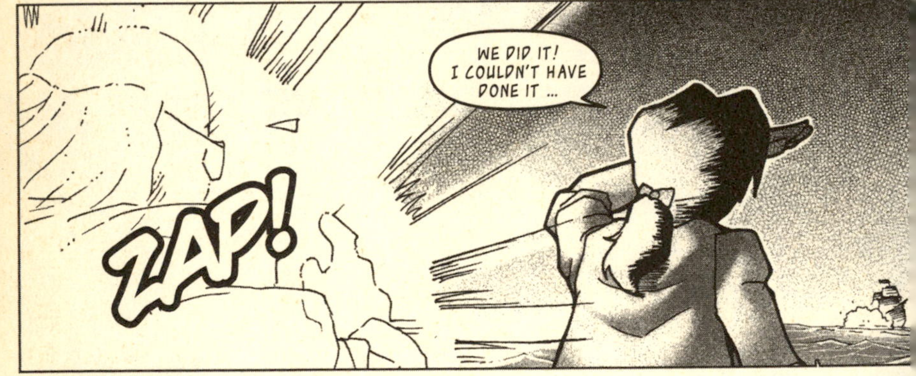
WE DID IT! I COULDN'T HAVE DONE IT ...
ZAP!

AND THINGS WERE GETTING WORSE ...
... WITHOUT ... YOU?
BENJAMIN?

WHAT HAPPENED?
WE WERE ATTACKED, SIR!
BY WHAT?
WE DO NOT KNOW!
THERE'S NOTHING OUT THERE!
NO MATTER!
FIRE AT WILL!!!
ALL HANDS!!! FIRE AT WILL!!!
... WITH EVERY PASSING SECOND.

AND WHERE WAS I?
... JUST USED A KNIFE, NO BOOKS, JUST LOOKING AT A POCKETWATCH.
I WANTED TO LEARN MORE ABOUT TIME AND HOW TIME WORKED.
OF COURSE, IT DIDN'T HELP.
I'VE ALWAYS BEEN INTERESTED IN HOW THINGS WORK.
HOW THE CLOCK WORKS ... HOW THE UNIVERSE WORKS ...

OUT THERE...
...THE WAY THE STARS SPIN AROUND, THE WAY OUR PLANET SPINS AROUND, THE WAY EVERYTHING SPINS AROUND ...
IT'S LIKE A GIANT CLOCK!

HMMMM, YOU MAY NOT LEARN MUCH ABOUT *TIME* WHEN YOU STUDY A CLOCK...

...BUT YOU *CAN* LEARN QUITE A BIT ABOUT THE CLOCKMAKER!
THAT CLOCK THERE SHOWS ME SO MUCH OF YOUR MIND AND YOUR HANDS AND, WELL, YOU!

MAYBE THAT'S WHY I LOVE STUDYING THE STARS SO MUCH THESE DAYS.
I'VE ALREADY LEARNED SO MUCH.
ONE DAY, I HOPE TO GET SOME BOOKS, A TELESCOPE ...

BUT I HAVE SO MUCH TO DO.
SINCE MY FATHER DIED, THE FARM HAS BEEN MY RESPONSIBILITY.
AND I HAVE TO TAKE CARE OF MY SISTERS AND MOTHER AND GRANDMOTHER ...

IT ALL COMES BACK TO TIME, DOESN'T IT?
NO TIME FOR ALL I WANT TO DO,
FOR ALL I NEED TO DO.
I WAS JUST CHATTING WITH MY NEW FRIEND, WHILE ONE OF MY OTHER FRIENDS ...

... WAS IN SERIOUS DANGER!
WE GOT AWAY FROM THE EXPLOSION IN TIME!
YEAH, TIME FOR A LITTLE REST.
KA-SPLOOSH!
WAM!
WHAT WAS THAT?
CANNON FIRE?
CANNON FIRE!?!
CANNON FIRE!!!

PEDAL!!!
I AM!!!
KA SPLOOSH!
KA SPLOOSH!
WELL, PEDAL FASTER!!!
I AM!!!

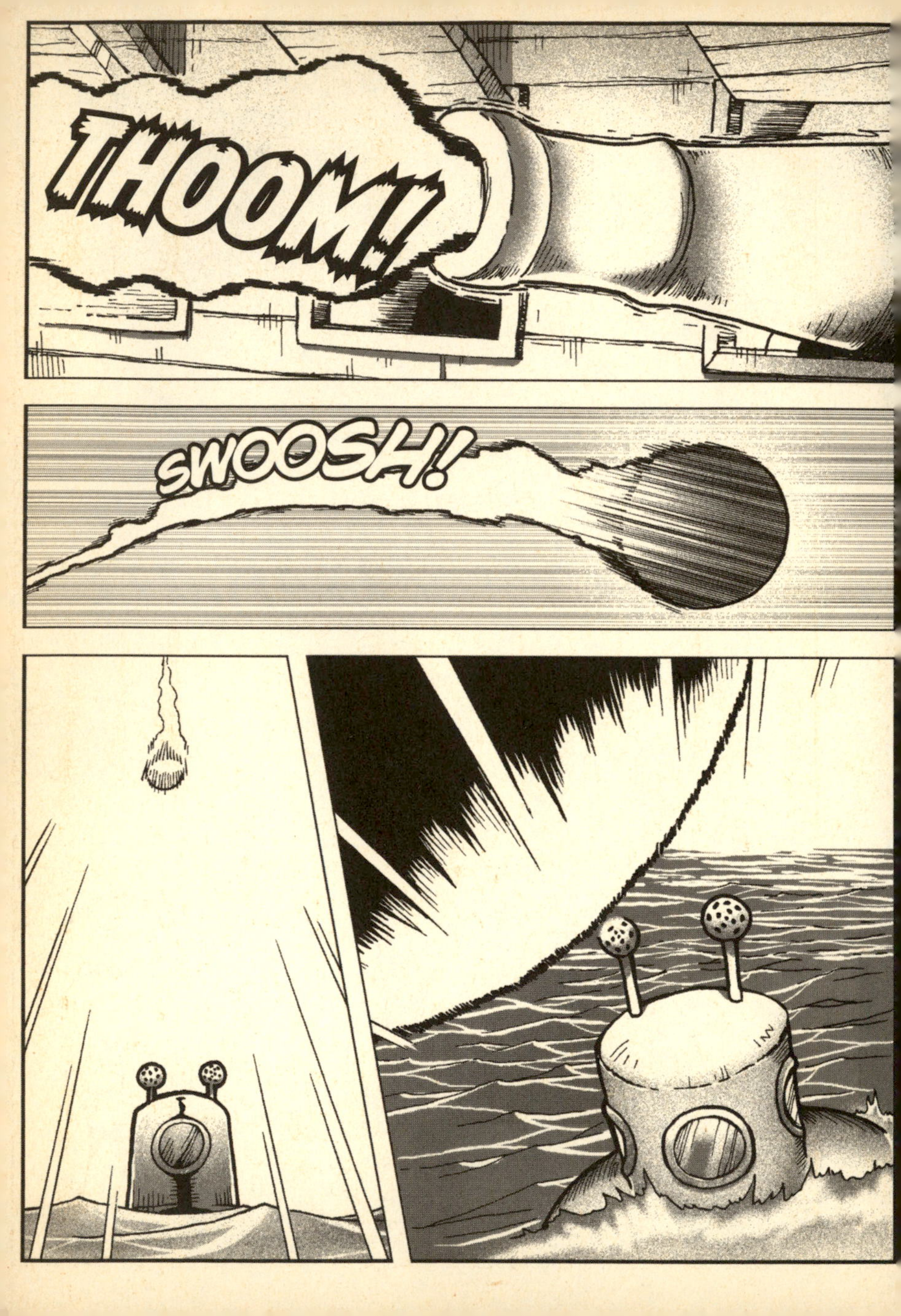
THOOM!
SWOOSH!

GOT IT ...
SPLUNK
NICE TEAMWORK!
I MAKE IT LIGHT AS A FEATHER, YOU HIT IT AWAY HARMLESSLY -- NO ONE GETS HURT!

RIGHT! NO ONE GETS HURT!
I'M GOING IN!
ANOTHER ONE?
NO ONE GETS HURT...

NO ONE GETS --
N.E.X.U.S.?
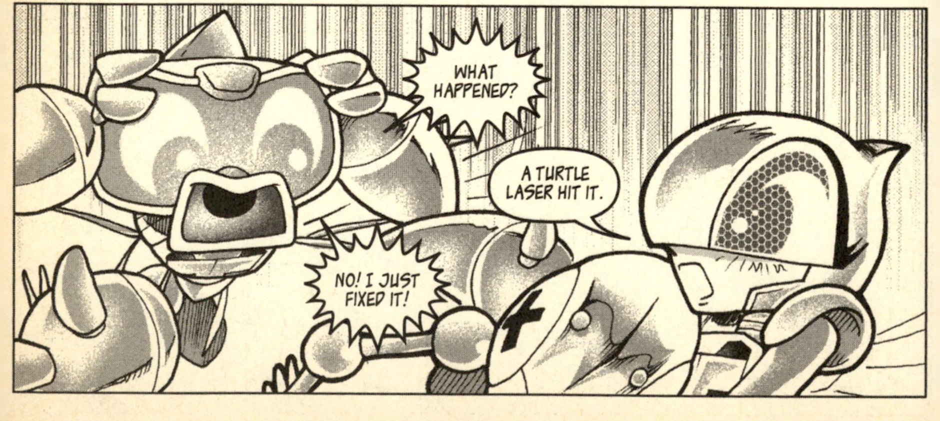
WHAT HAPPENED?
A TURTLE LASER HIT IT.
NO! I JUST FIXED IT!

WE'VE GOT TO GET OUT OF HERE!
WHILE WE STILL CAN!

NO WAY!
WE AREN'T LEAVING SERGEANT LEE HERE ALONE!
I CAN'T TAKE YOU BOTH THROUGH A WORMHOLE! I SPENT TOO MUCH ENERGY FIXING YOUR TURTLES!

NOPE!
NOT UNTIL WE RESCUE SERGEANT LEE!
YEAH! YEAH! NOT UNTIL YOU RESCUE SERGEANT LEE!

FINE.

ARE THEY IN THERE?
YES.
SO WHY ARE THEY STILL IN THERE?
WE HAVE TO RESCUE SERGEANT LEE.

ZAP!
OH YEAH -- THAT!
BOINK!

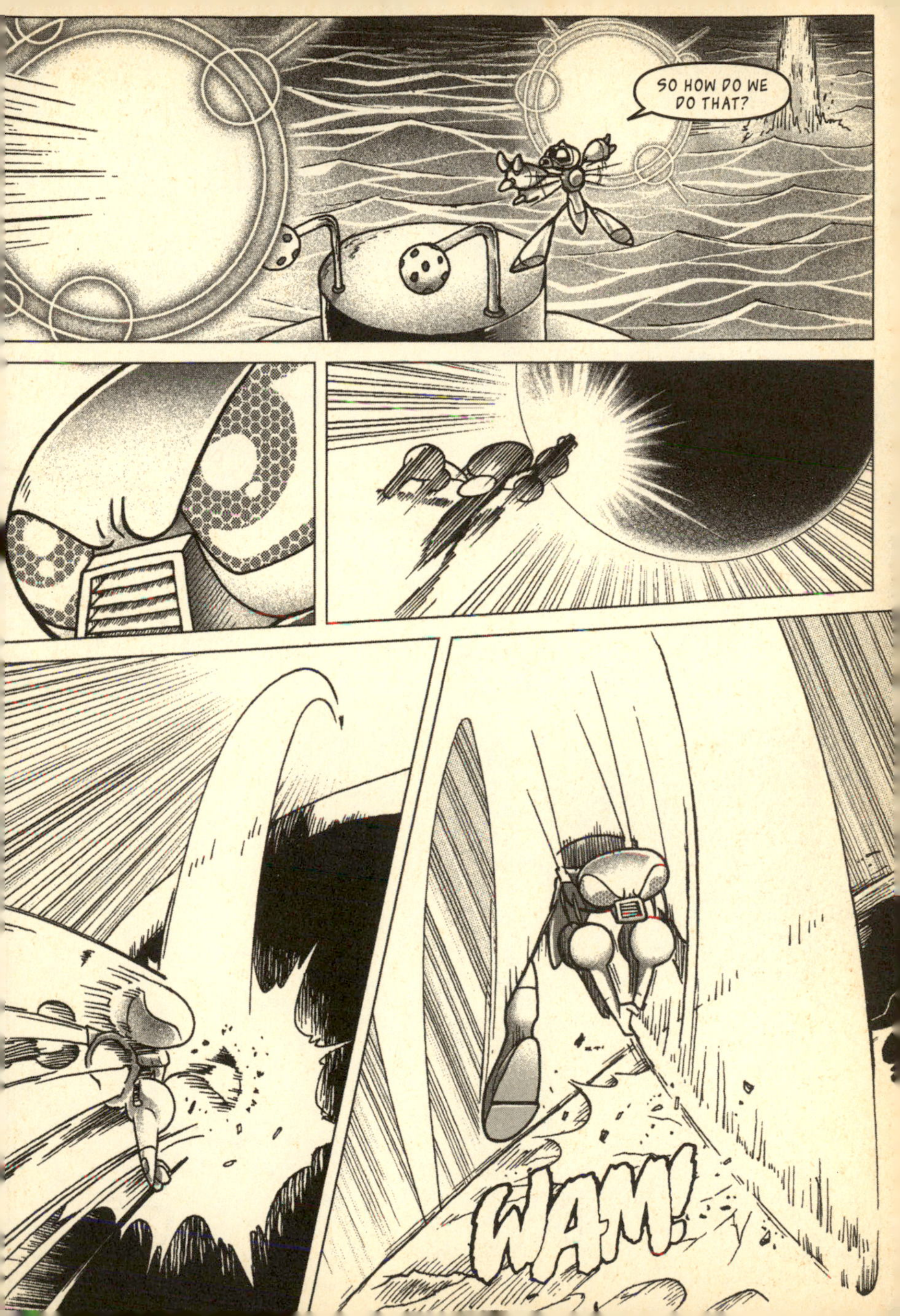
SO HOW DO WE DO THAT?
WAM!

YEAH, WE COULD KEEP DOING THIS ... IT'S KIND OF FUN ...
KEEP GOING!!!
MY FRIENDS ARE TAKING CARE OF THE REST!!!
WHY?
I DON'T LIKE YOU, AND YOU DON'T LIKE ME? WHAT'S IN IT FOR YOU?
I DON'T THINK YOU'D UNDERSTAND ...

GOODNESS!
IT WORKED! YOU MADE IT!
SERGEANT LEE?
CLANG!

WHAT HAPPENED?
YOU WOULDN'T BELIEVE ME IF'N I TOLD YA.
DON'T RIGHTLY BELIEVE MY OWN SELF!

ELF-FAIRY GIRL! ALL GROWED UP AGAIN!
WHAT?

MR. BUSHNELL, WHERE IS MR. FRANKLIN?
HE'S LEFT, YOUNG LADY.
ONE MOMENT HE WAS HERE, THE NEXT HE WAS NOT.
OH NO.

KINDA ... LIKE ... THAT ...
DON'T WORRY, MR. BUSHNELL, THIS HAS BEEN A NIGHT OF STRANGE HAPPENINGS.
IT'LL BE OKAY.
WHAT?
I'M JUST WAITING FOR THE INSULT TO FOLLOW. WHAT HAPPENED TO YOU OUT THERE?
I TOLD YOU, YOU WOULDN'T BELIEVE IF'N I TOLD YA!

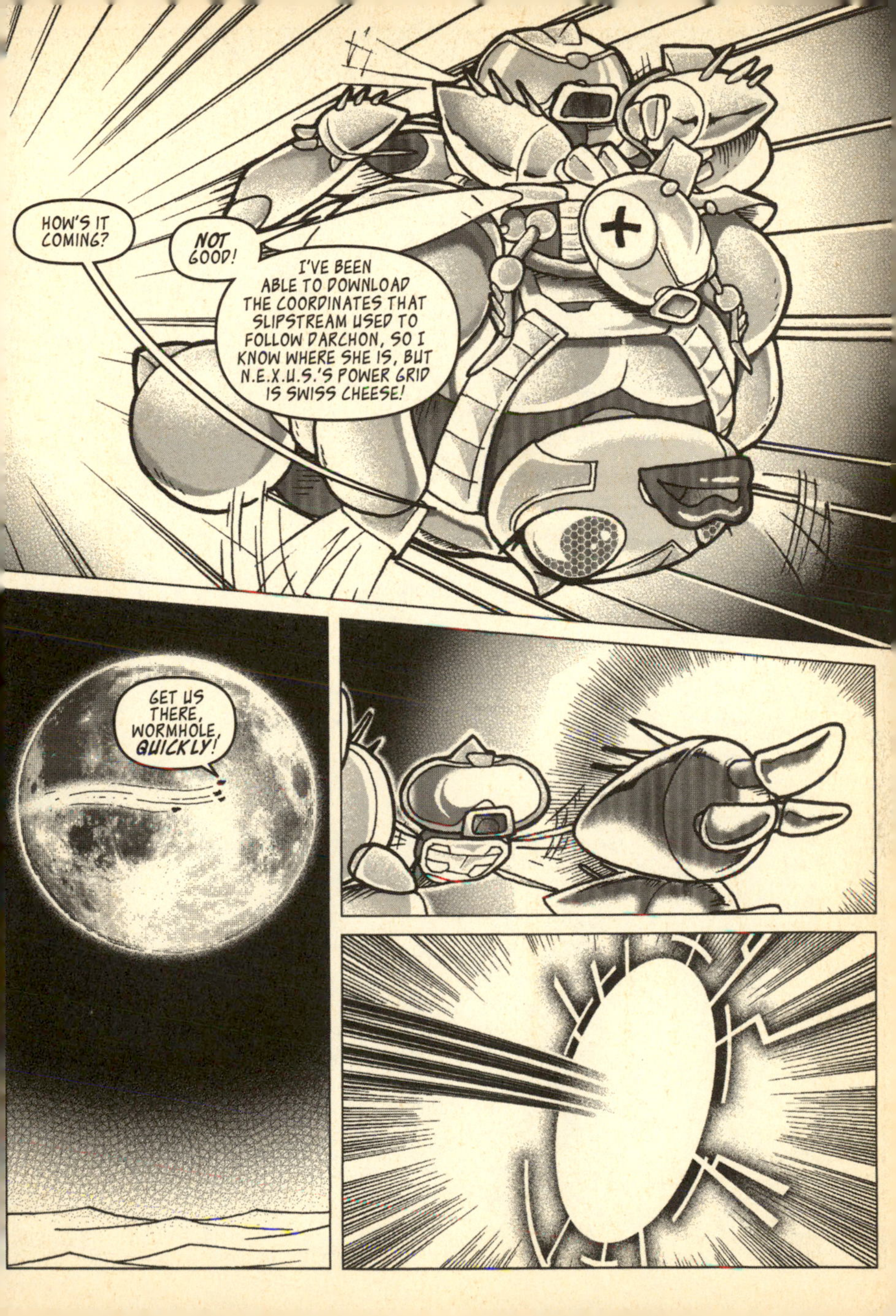
HOW'S IT COMING?
NOT GOOD!
I'VE BEEN ABLE TO DOWNLOAD THE COORDINATES THAT SLIPSTREAM USED TO FOLLOW DARCHON, SO I KNOW WHERE SHE IS, BUT N.E.X.U.S.'S POWER GRID IS SWISS CHEESE!
GET US THERE, WORMHOLE, QUICKLY!

MY GRANDMOTHER TAUGHT ME HOW TO READ USING HER BIBLE.
YOU TALKED ABOUT GETTING TO KNOW THE CLOCKMAKER ...
HOLY BIBLE
I READ THINGS LIKE, "FOR I KNOW THE THOUGHTS THAT I THINK TOWARD YOU, SAITH THE LORD, THOUGHTS OF PEACE, AND NOT OF EVIL, TO GIVE YOU AN EXPECTED END."
THE STARS TELL US THE CLOCKMAKER IS POWERFUL.
AND THIS TELLS US THAT AS POWERFUL AS HE IS, HE CARES ABOUT US.

THAT KIND OF THING IS COMFORTING WHILE WAITING TO BE KIDNAPPED BY AN EVIL TIME-TRAVELING SPIDER.
YES, I WOULD IMAGINE SO ...

WORMHOLE?
MOTHER MASS?
TAK?

DARCHON TOOK BENJAMIN FRANKLIN, WE THINK, AND --
-- OH DEAR --
--I'M GETTING TRACES OF A QUANTUM SIGNATURE -- DARCHON'S SIGNATURE!

HE'S ALREADY LEFT!

LET'S MOVE, EVERYONE!
WE'VE GOT TO FOLLOW --
NO USE, MA'AM ...

I CAN'T GET N.E.X.U.S. TO FULL CAPACITY ...
WE CAN'T FOLLOW, AND THE TRAIL HAS ALREADY GROWN COLD ...

THEN ...
... WE'VE FAILED ...
AND ALL MY WORST FEARS CAME TRUE.

WHAT DO YOU MEAN, SLIPSTREAM?
HELLO, LAUREL TEMPLETON. NICE TO SEE YOU AGAIN!
HI!
WHO ARE YOU?
WE CAN'T FOLLOW DARCHON UNTIL N.E.X.U.S. IS REPAIRED ...
BUT IT WILL TAKE TOO LONG TO REPAIR IT, AND HE COULD BE ANYWHERE IN INFINITY, NOW.
AND WE HAVE NO WAY OF KNOWING WHERE OR WHEN ...
ALL MY WORK, ALL MY PLANNING, ALL MY EFFORT ... ENDED ... IN FAILURE ...

MAYBE NOT.

WHAT IF YOU KNEW EXACTLY WHERE AND WHEN HE WOULD STRIKE?
COULD YOU JUST GO STRAIGHT THERE WITHOUT HAVING TO FOLLOW HIM?

YOU CAME AND VISITED ME THE SAME TIME THAT SPIDER DID, ALL THOSE YEARS AGO.
JUST BEFORE YOU CAME, I HAD TAKEN SOME OF THE GEARS OUT OF THIS WATCH, ONE LAST TIME, TO COMPARE THEM TO SOME GEARS I HAD CARVED.
I PUT IT BACK TOGETHER, HOPING I COULD GIVE IT BACK TO THE MAN WHO LOANED IT TO ME.

BUT AFTER THE EXCITEMENT, I NEVER WOUND IT UP AGAIN ...
... NEVER NEEDED TO.
TUESDAY, OCTOBER 16, 1753.
ELEVEN ON THE CLOCK AND FORTY-THREE MINUTES.

THAT ENOUGH FOR YOU TO WORK ON?
MORE THAN ENOUGH!

WE CAN JUST TAKE OUR TIME, NOW!
I CAN FINALLY TAKE THE TIME TO FIX N.E.X.U.S. RIGHT!

WELL, YOU HAVE ALMOST ALL THE TIME IN THE WORLD, NOW, SINCE WE KNOW EXACTLY WHERE DARCHON IS GOING TO BE!

CHAPTER seven

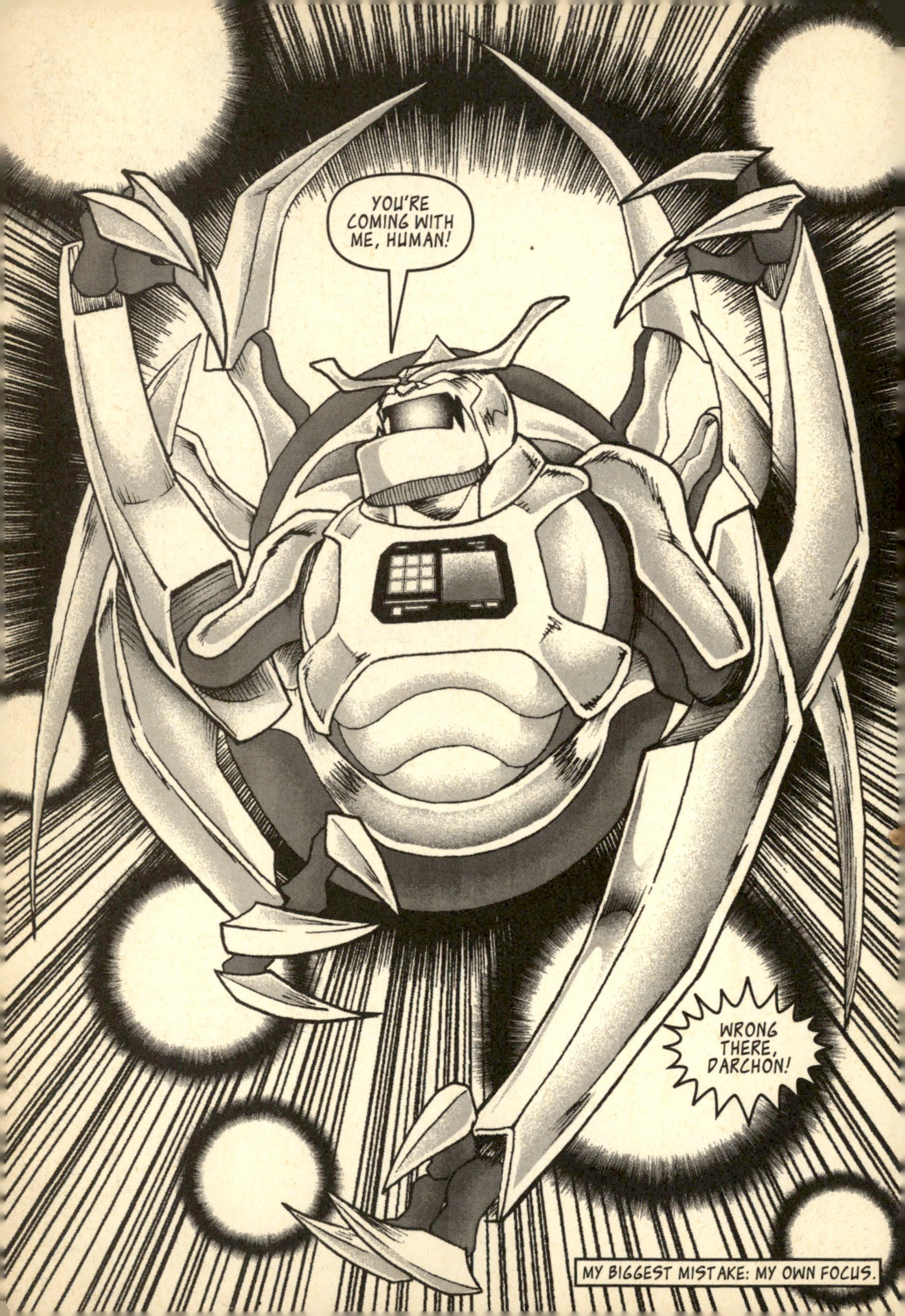
YOU'RE COMING WITH ME, HUMAN!
WRONG THERE, DARCHON!
MY BIGGEST MISTAKE: MY OWN FOCUS.

NO!
IT'S NOT POSSIBLE!
I WORRIED SO MUCH ...
YOU CAN SAY THAT IF YOU LIKE!
BUT POSSIBLE OR IMPOSSIBLE, IT HAPPENED AND WE'RE HERE TO STOP YOU!
... TRIED TO DO IT ALL ...

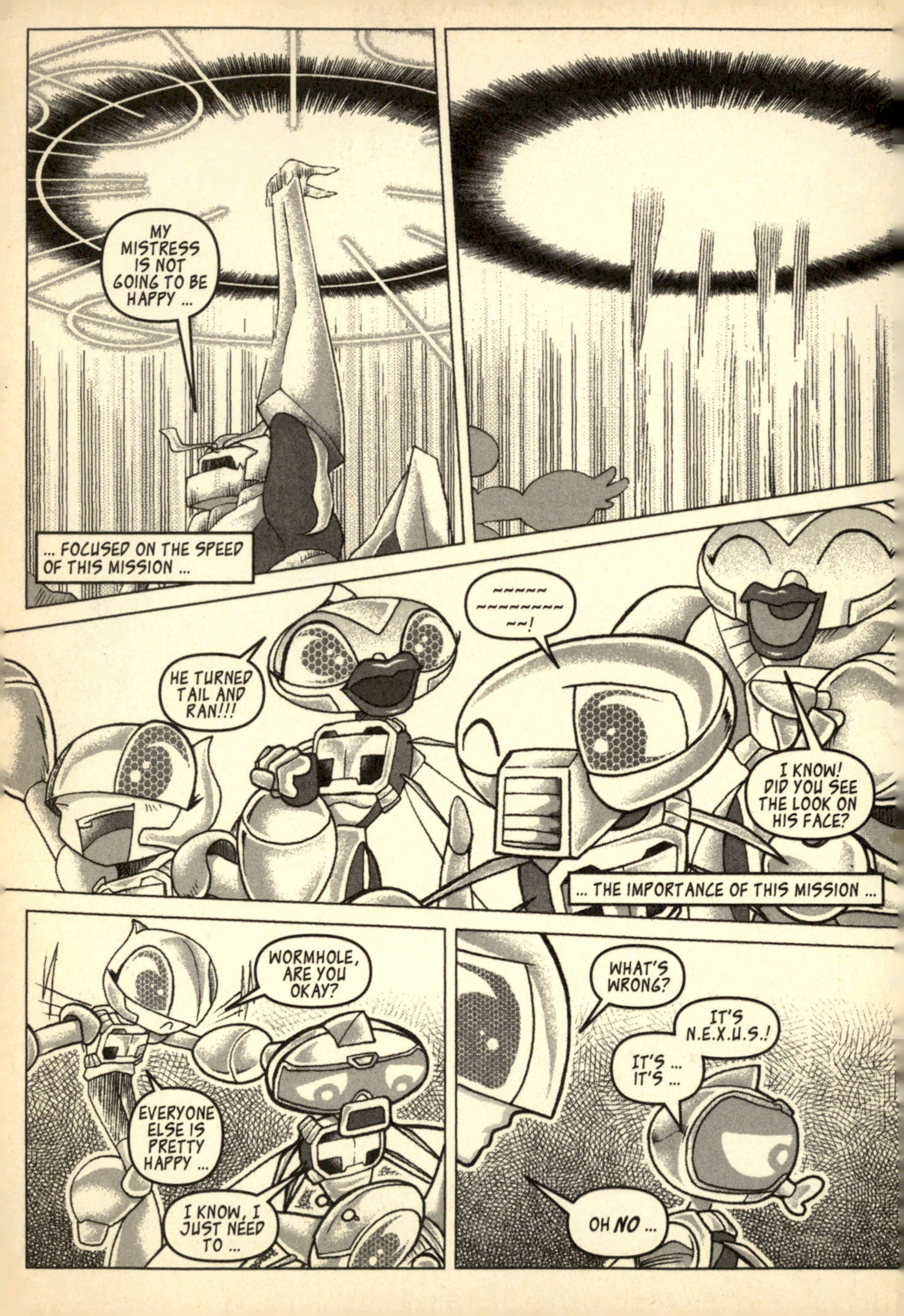
MY MISTRESS IS NOT GOING TO BE HAPPY ...
... FOCUSED ON THE SPEED OF THIS MISSION ...
HE TURNED TAIL AND RAN!!!
~~~~~ ~~~~~~~~~ ~~!
I KNOW! DID YOU SEE THE LOOK ON HIS FACE?
... THE IMPORTANCE OF THIS MISSION ...
WORMHOLE, ARE YOU OKAY?
EVERYONE ELSE IS PRETTY HAPPY ...
I KNOW, I JUST NEED TO ...
WHAT'S WRONG?
IT'S N.E.X.U.S.!
IT'S ... IT'S ...
OH NO ...
~~~~~

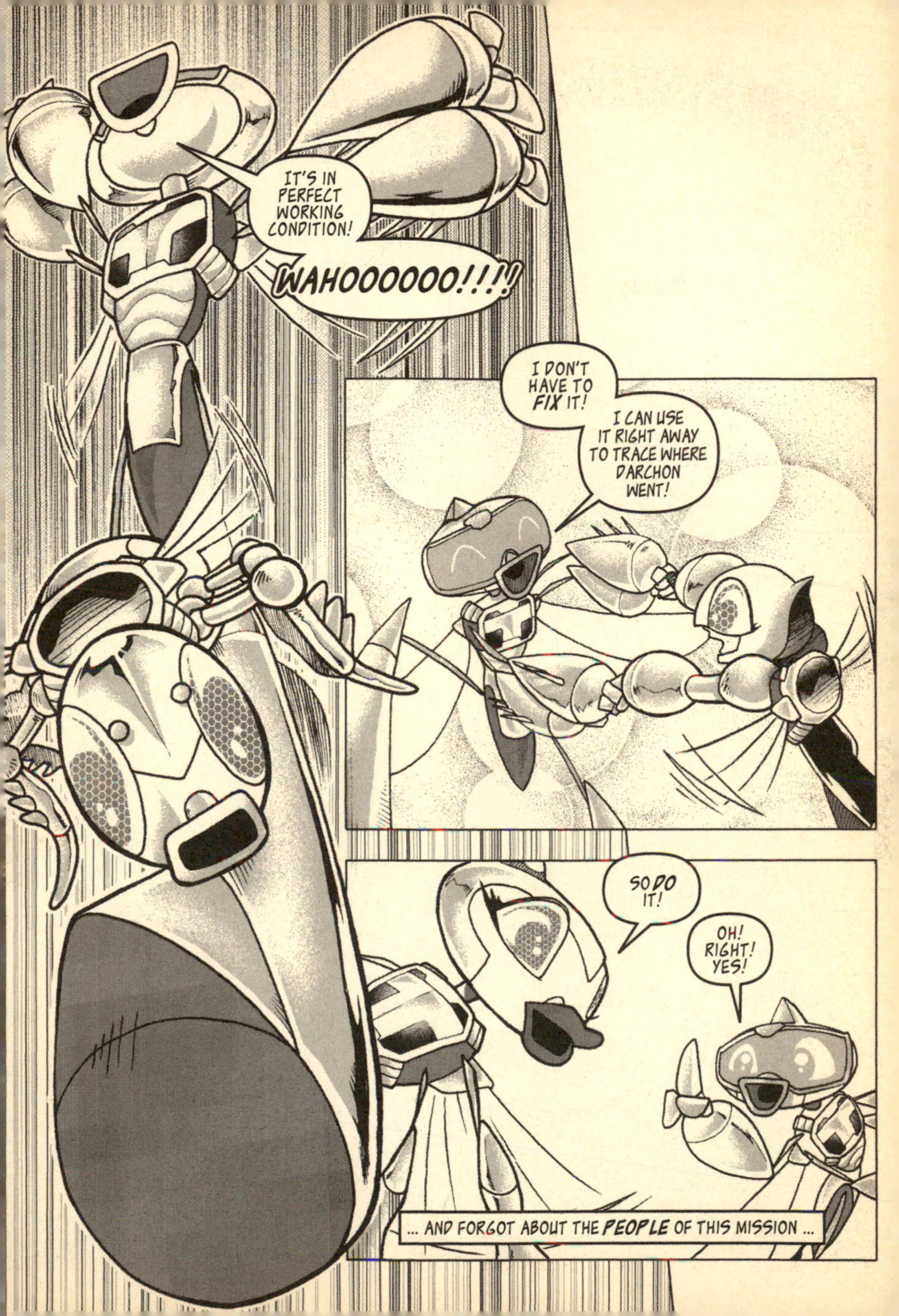
IT'S IN PERFECT WORKING CONDITION!
WAHOOOOOO!!!!
I DON'T HAVE TO FIX IT!
I CAN USE IT RIGHT AWAY TO TRACE WHERE DARCHON WENT!
SO DO IT!
OH! RIGHT! YES!
... AND FORGOT ABOUT THE PEOPLE OF THIS MISSION ...

HELLO, MR. BANNEKER.
IT'S GOOD TO SEE YOU AGAIN.
AGAIN?
... AND THE "CLOCKMAKER."

I ... WHAT ... WHO ...?
HEHEH, THIS MAY BE A LOT TO TAKE IN. ALLOW ME TO INTRODUCE YOU TO MY FRIENDS.
NOT BENJAMIN BANNEKER ...

HI!
I'M LAUREL! LAUREL TEMPLETON!
... BUT THE CLOCKMAKER WHO "KNOWS THE PLANS HE HAS FOR US ..."

UH, WORMHOLE, I, UH, GOT SOMETHING TO SAY ...
... WHO WOUND THE UNIVERSE, SETTING EVERY PARTICLE INTO MOTION ...

YEAH?
... INFINITE PARTICLES THAT MAKE UP INFINITE COMBINATIONS ...

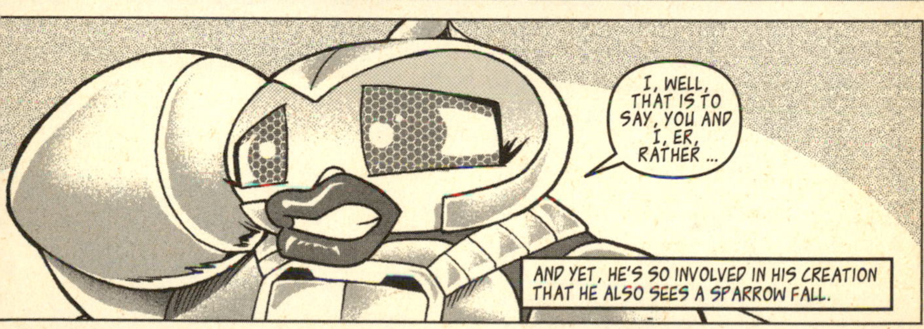
I, WELL, THAT IS TO SAY, YOU AND I, ER, RATHER ...
AND YET, HE'S SO INVOLVED IN HIS CREATION THAT HE ALSO SEES A SPARROW FALL.

YOU KNOW, AND SO, WE ...
... AND I, WELL, HAVE TO SAY THAT, I HAVEN'T, SOMETIMES, UH ...
YOU KNOW WHAT I MEAN?

I DO.
THANKS.
I WAS SO WORRIED ABOUT THE BIG PICTURE, I FORGOT ABOUT THE DETAILS.
AND I PUT ALL THAT RESPONSIBILITY ON MY FOUR SHOULDERS, FORGETTING THAT I NOT ONLY HAD A TEAM TO HELP ME ...
ALMOST READY TO GO, WORMHOLE?
JUST ABOUT, SLIPSTREAM.
WE'RE READY TO GO AS SOON AS YOU ARE.

... I HAD A FAMILY.